The School of Life

Rachel Ambat
Illustrated by Emily Reich

Dedicated to my Heavenly Father:
Thank you, Heavenly Father, for loving me and saving me. I thank you for your School of Life, where you take me as I am and mold me to be more like you. You are truly such a wonderful teacher and father to me, and I love you very much.

Dedicated to my dearest sister, Christina Ambat:
Thank you so much for the many ideas and love and the encouragement that made this book what it is. You mean so much to me, and I am so glad to have a sister like you.

Contents

Author's note:

Hello, my dear friend! Welcome to the School of Life! It is my heart's desire that through the course of this book, you will draw closer to our Heavenly Father and know how much He loves you. He loves you so much that He was willing to die on the cross for you so that you could live eternally with Him. I pray that you will take with you a special lesson from each story that can only be taught in the School of Life. I am so delighted that you have chosen to embark on this special journey with me, and I hope that you will be blessed.

Are you ready to get started? Let's begin and read a story that happened long ago and continues to happen today.

With love and prayers for you, my special friend,

Rachel

Chapter One: What Would Jesus Do?

"Whoever says he abides in him ought to walk in the same way in which he walked." 1 John 2:6

Miss Jane sat at her desk and gazed dreamily at the classroom in front of her which would soon be filled with students. Her greatest ambition was that each one of her students would come to know Jesus as their personal Savior and would form a deep relationship with Him. Getting up from her seat, she went over to each desk and prayed for the student who would sit there. "O Lord," she prayed, "touch these children's lives in a special way, and let them feel your love in this classroom. In this upcoming year, help us to follow you and make friendships for life."

****

It seemed like just a few minutes before the quiet classroom was filled with the cheerful voices of friends greeting those whom they had missed over the summer. Children of different backgrounds filled the little classroom. Miss Jane cheerfully welcomed each student back.

The schoolteacher noticed a few new faces in classroom. One new student was a girl who had bright golden hair and sweet blue eyes. She sat in the corner of the room, eyeing each student in a somewhat snobbish manner. Miss Jane saw her and wondered if perhaps she was staring because she was decked in beautiful clothing and the others were dressed in plain, everyday clothes. Miss Jane had noticed that she took special care not to let the ends of her dress touch the floor and walked on her tiptoes so that not much of her shiny black boots would get dirty.

Miss Jane looked across the room and beheld the sight of a boy who was just the opposite of the girl. He was dressed in clothing that was rather old, although clean, and was wearing a pair of sorrowful-looking, torn old shoes. "The poor boy," Miss Jane thought. The boy would take no notice of anybody but just sat alone and sulked. "He would look quite handsome if he smiled," said Miss Jane to herself. "I daresay he'll have something to smile about before the year is over. Still, he looks like a tough one to manage."

She looked over to the second new boy and was relieved to see that he seemed quite different compared to the other two new students. He was a jolly-looking thing with sparkling big green eyes, red hair, and freckles on his brown skin. However, when Miss Jane saw a frog with big, bulging eyes peek out of his pocket and the boy hurriedly push it back down, she thought, "He seems nice, but he can certainly be a bit of a monkey. I best get ready for a whole truckload of mischief."

After studying each student a little while longer, Miss Jane smiled and thought to herself, "Well, I don't know exactly what this year will bring, but I do know one thing—this year certainly won't be dull!"

Miss Jane clapped her hands. "Take your seats, class," she said. There was a sudden scurrying as everyone ran to sit in the seat they liked the best. Miss Jane waited till the shuffling of feet ceased and the students settled down. Then she began.

"My name is Miss Jane, and I will be your teacher this year." She looked around. "Most of you know me, as I taught you all last year. I welcome those of you who are new this year. I am very glad that you are here, and I hope that you will grow in your faith while attending this school. I hope you will come to know Christ as your personal Savior and that you will know how much He loves you."

"No offense," said the sulky-looking boy, "but not everyone believes in that sort of religion."

Miss Jane turned around and looked at him. She said kindly, "If you wish to dispute the matter, please talk to me after class. And I'd appreciate it if, in the future, you'd raise your hand and wait for me to call on you before you speak. Do you understand?" The boy nodded and relapsed into his sullen mood. Miss Jane sighed quietly.

"Let's begin with attendance," she said, pulling out her list of names. "When I call on you, I want you to raise your hand and tell us a little bit about yourself so the new students get to know you. Then, I want you to tell us something fun that you did this summer. Let's begin."

Attendance went smoothly. The girl with the golden hair and blue eyes introduced herself as Priscilla Robinson. Priscilla was quite disturbed at being addressed by just her first name. She said that their butler called her *Miss* Priscilla and wanted all the students to do the same. The sulky-looking boy, whose name was Abel, ignored Miss Jane completely, and she told him to see her after class. The boy with the red hair and green eyes was Patrick, but he said that everyone called him Pat.

After attendance, the class did Bible reading and prayer, which Abel seemed to hate. Priscilla, on the other hand, said that she was quite used to doing the things "good people" did. They then went on to Mathematics, an hour which proved to be very chaotic.

Miss Jane was writing sums on the board, and the class was copying them down on their slates. Now, Pat was rather bored, for he wasn't very fond of Math. He couldn't stop himself from looking at Priscilla, who was playing with her hair instead of doing the Math problems. He choked back gurgles of laughter. "How ridiculous she looks!" he thought to himself. "She thinks so highly of herself. Why does she pay so much attention to her looks? As if anyone would notice if her hair was a bird's nest and she had twenty spots on her face! She's too vain to look at."

Pat's frog stuck his head out of Pat's pocket, and Pat hurriedly pushed it back. Then, a marvelous idea started forming in Pat's little red head. "I bet Miss Robinson would hate

Prissy let out a chilling scream

having a dirty little frog jump on her clean frock. Wouldn't that be funny? I'd just love to see 'Miss Dignified' give a yell!"

Pat realized that his desk was too far from Prissy, so he passed his frog to a boy named Charlie. He signed to Charlie to put the frog on Prissy's desk when it was her turn to solve the sums on the board.

The boys watched with nervous excitement as Prissy walked back to her desk. She didn't notice the frog at first, but Pat's frog soon decided he liked the look of Prissy, and with one huge bound, he leaped onto her lap. Prissy let out a chilling scream and brushed the frog quickly from her lap.

Miss Jane looked up with a startled face. "Priscilla, whatever is the matter?"

"Oh, Miss Jane, that wicked boy put a frog on my desk!" cried Priscilla, pointing a finger at Charlie, who was sitting right next to her.

"Where is the frog now?" asked Miss Jane.

"I don't know," said Priscilla, beginning to sob.

Miss Jane began walking over to her, then stopped suddenly. Something was climbing up her leg! Miss Jane pulled up her skirt, and there was the huge frog, clinging to her! Miss Jane exclaimed in surprise and shook the frog off her. The frog fell to the ground, and quickly, Miss Jane grabbed a shovel, scooped it up, and threw the naughty frog outside.

Miss Jane returned to the classroom, trying to look calm. She immediately saw Pat's guilty face and said, "Pat, perhaps you are responsible for this?"

"No, it was that wicked boy," cried Priscilla, pointing at Charlie. When neither of the boys said anything, Miss Jane said, "Both of you, see me after class," and both boys answered, "Yes, Miss Jane."

The class went smoothly after that, with no more episodes. Finally, Miss Jane looked at the clock and said "Lunch!" "Oh, boy!" cried the students, grabbing their lunch pails. They opened the classroom door and ran outside. They liked to eat and have recess in the schoolyard when the weather was nice.

"Charlie and Pat, please stay behind," said Miss Jane. The boys looked at each other and then at the floor. When everyone was gone, Miss Jane gave them the dreaded talk, which went straight to the hearts of both the boys.

"Please tell me what happened, without leaving out any detail," she said. So the boys related everything, feeling very guilty and rather foolish.

"So it was your idea, Pat," said Miss Jane at the end. "And Charlie helped you carry it out."

Pat nodded miserably. "I'm really sorry, Miss Jane," he said. "I knew it was wrong. It just seemed like such a marvelous idea at that time."

"But why did you do it?"

"It's just that Prissy thinks so much of herself because she's rich, and she thinks so lowly of us just because we're not. I wanted to get back at her for being so haughty and mean and freak her out."

"And you did," said Miss Jane, giving what her students called the 'conviction stare.'

"It's just not fair," said Charlie, "that some people have so much while others have so little."

"But you have so much, Charlie," said Miss Jane. "In fact, you have something worth more than all the riches of this world combined."

"I do? What is it, Miss Jane?"

"Jesus," answered Miss Jane, smiling at him. "And you are so blessed to have Him as your Lord and Savior. Don't you think?"

"Yeah!" said Charlie, grinning. "I never thought of it like that before, Miss Jane!"

"Me neither," said Pat. "You know, I'm a Christian, too. I invited Jesus into my heart last summer."

"Oh, really!" said Miss Jane, pretending to be shocked. "Well then, you must try to be like Jesus more and more every day. You didn't do very well today. Do you think Jesus would plan on scaring his classmate with a frog?"

"No," said Pat, looking down at the floor.

"I didn't think so either. Pat and Charlie, since you both follow Jesus, you must ask yourself before doing anything, 'What would Jesus do?' Do you understand?"

"Yes, Miss Jane," replied the boys.

"It's just so hard," said Pat, "to always remember that."

"Indeed it is. But we have Jesus to help and guide us every day. I feel sorry for people who don't know Jesus and have to bear their trials and their burdens all by themselves."

"Like Priscilla?" asked Charlie.

"We can't know for sure," said Miss Jane. "Only God knows the heart. But if Priscilla is one of those people, then we need to make sure we tell her the good news. We should also pray for her and be kind to her, for things must be pretty hard on her."

"We will, Miss Jane," said the boys. "We'll be kind to Priscilla and pray for her. We'll tell her the good news."

"That's my boys," said Miss Jane, patting them. "Always remember that when the road gets rough, we can always come to our Father who is waiting to help, guide, and love His children."

"We'll remember, Miss Jane," said the boys. "We'll remember."

And they did.

Chapter Two: Spreading the Good News

"And he said to them, Go into all the world, and proclaim the gospel to the whole creation." Mark 16:15

The first thing Charlie and Pat did to be kind to Priscilla was give her a letter apologizing for what they had done to her in class. She received it with a haughty air and said, "How can I forgive you for such abominable behavior? I don't believe impolite boys like you would write an apology letter on your own accord, anyway. Miss Jane probably made you. I can't believe I'm going to school with such bad-mannered boys!" And with a toss of her golden hair, she left the boys feeling rather injured and downcast. "Well, I don't care what she does!" said Pat. "We did the right thing, and we should still be nice to her because that's what Jesus would do!"

"You're right," said Charlie. "But I can't help feeling a little hurt at being called a bad-mannered boy."

The boys persevered in doing nice things for Priscilla. When she needed help with her homework, the boys gave it. When her favorite pencil broke, Pat gave her one of his. When she lost her bracelet, the boys looked all over the school grounds to help her find it. The boys found it difficult to be nice to her at first, but as they persisted, it became easier. They each remembered to pray for her every night as well.

Without realizing it, Priscilla started to like the boys. She began confiding in them and depending on them whenever she needed help. She felt sure something was different about them. They were not like other people. They had something that she did not, and she began to long for what they had.

One sunny day, Pat and Charlie decided to go to Priscilla's house after school. They brought with them a pail of homemade cookies and some freshly squeezed lemonade. The boys had decided to share the gospel with Priscilla that day. Charlie brought a Bible in which Pat had bookmarked all the pages containing the important verses that they were going to use for their witnessing. Both the boys were rather nervous, but they had prayed and asked God to speak to Priscilla's heart. So, they went out in faith.

Priscilla's house was enormous, and the boys gaped at it in wonder. When Charlie rang the bell, the butler answered the door.

"Good afternoon. We are here to see Priscilla," they said politely.

"She's in the backyard," replied the butler, letting them in and directing them to the yard.

When Charlie and Pat reached the backyard, they found Priscilla sitting in the shade under a tree. To their surprise, she was crying!

"Priscilla, what's the matter?" they asked, running to comfort her. Priscilla's tear-stained face looked up, startled to see them.

"Oh, nothing," she said quickly, trying to wipe away her tears.

"No, something's wrong," said Charlie. "You can tell us Prissy. We're your friends."

Priscilla looked up into Pat and Charlie's kind faces. Then she burst into tears.

"It's just...it's just that I miss my parents so much. They're so busy all the time. They travel often and hardly spend any time with me. The butler and my nanny are family friends and they take good care of me and make sure that I have everything I need, but I'd rather have my parents. Even now, my father's gone on a business trip to Europe, and my mother is with him. I don't even know when they'll be coming back! I miss having someone to talk to."

"Poor Prissy," said Pat, feeling terribly sorry for her. "Well, we have just the right thing to cheer you up!"

They presented the cookies and the lemonade and were glad to hear Priscilla laugh. "You guys are always so kind," said Prissy thankfully. "A lot kinder than I am. I try to get everyone to think I'm rich and have everything I want. But the truth is, I don't."

Pat and Charlie nodded their heads understandingly.

"Why are you guys so different from everyone else?" asked Priscilla. "You are always so kind to me, even when I am dreadfully rude."

"Except for the frog episode," said Pat, ashamed.

Priscilla grinned. "I rather deserved it though, didn't I?"

Pat and Charlie smiled. "You're seeing Jesus in us, Prissy," they said. "This is what Jesus does. He makes us love and be kind to others, even when they are not nice to us. He's a friend when you have no one. He's worth more than silver, or gold, or anything this world has to offer. He loves everyone, including you."

"Tell me more about Jesus," said Prissy eagerly.

So, the boys told Prissy the whole gospel story and what Jesus did for her.

Then they asked her, "Do you want to accept Jesus as your Savior and Lord, and do you want to follow him?"

"Yes!" cried Priscilla, her face filled with joy.

****

Meanwhile, Miss Jane was talking to Abel about Jesus as well. She had prayed so hard that God would soften Abel's heart and that he would listen. To her surprise, Abel did listen, although he said, "You can try Miss Jane, but I don't think you'll be able to get me to believe that sort of religion." Miss Jane shared with him the gospel, showing him Bible verse after Bible verse. "Do you believe now, Abel?" she asked when she had finished. "I don't know, Miss Jane," said Abel doubtfully. "There might be something in it after all. I see that believing in Jesus makes people act differently. You and all the other kids here act way different than the people at my other school. I've just gone through a lot of things in my life to make me doubt...and if you don't mind, I'd like to think about it for a little while."

"Of course, Abel," said Miss Jane.

****

It was very early in the morning. There were two hours left before school began. A young boy walked into town with an anxious expression on his face. Going into the department store, he asked if there were any letters for him.

"Yep. There's one for Abel Blackstone," said the clerk. "Here you are." The boy snatched the letter and read it. It was a letter from his mother.

****

Miss Jane was sitting at her desk correcting papers when she heard a knock.

"Come in," called Miss Jane. She was surprised to see Abel. "Abel, what are you doing here so early?" she asked.

"Miss Jane," started Abel, "you know how yesterday I said I still wasn't sure I believed in God?"

"Yes."

"Well, here's why. A couple of years ago, my mom left me without even saying goodbye. I was devastated and angry... angry with myself and at God. I thought it was my fault that my mom left, but I also thought God could have stopped her from leaving. I stopped going to church and Sunday school because I didn't believe God cared about me...I didn't believe anyone cared about me. But yesterday, when you took the time to talk to me even after I gave you a pretty hard time about it...well, after feeling so lonely like I did, it was nice to think that maybe...maybe..." Abel stopped, looking slightly embarrassed.

Miss Jane smiled. "Abel," she said in a soft voice that made the boy look up at her kind face, "I can't imagine how difficult things were for you when your mom left. But I care about you...and so does Jesus."

Abel felt sudden tears spring into his eyes, but he blinked them back and mustered a smile. "After coming to this school, I see that you and the people who believe in Jesus are different from the ones who don't," he continued. "They're more kind, more…loving. When you told me about Jesus yesterday, I should have believed what you said. I tried not to, but last night, I kept thinking about everything, and I couldn't fall asleep. What if God was showing that He cared about me by having you speak to me? The thought kept coming into my head, and I prayed, 'God, if you're there and you truly do see me and care about me…please, could you show me one more time?' Earlier today, I went to the department store in town and asked if there was a letter for me. You see, I've always clung to a small hope that I might get word from my mother one day. Today, I was surprised beyond words, because inside an envelope, was a whole page-long letter from my mother. She said that this summer, she had accepted Jesus as her Lord and Savior. She also said that she was sorry she left me and that she was blinded by anger. She said that Jesus changed her, and she feels like a different person. She's praying for me and hopes that one day I'd be able to forgive her for how she hurt me." Abel's eyes brightened. "Miss Jane, I believe now that Jesus really does care for me. And I believe He is God because He alone can change others and heal broken hearts. I…I'm sorry I didn't believe you when you told me about Him yesterday. But now I do, and I want to learn more about Him. Could you…could you help me?"

"Of course, Abel," Miss Jane said with a joyous smile, her heart filled with happiness. "I would love too."

And so, in that small little classroom, Abel learned of a God who wanted more than anything for him to accept Christ as his Savior and become His child; of a God who left everything in heaven to come to earth and save him; of a God who did care about Abel…so much so, that He stretched out His arms on a cross to prove just how much.

Chapter Three: Confess That Mess!

"I acknowledged my sin to you, and I did not cover my iniquity; I said, I will confess my transgressions to the LORD, and you forgave the iniquity of my sin." Psalm 32:5

Prissy sat in the garden, feeling very bored. Pat and Charlie usually visited her regularly, but they were away on a vacation. It was her nanny's day off, and the butler was in his office, working. The maids were busy doing their Saturday cleaning and would not allow Prissy to help them. Prissy had begged them to let her, but they thought the little girl would only get in their way. The cook was making something special for dinner and would allow no one to enter her kitchen. Prissy sighed. She wished someone would just come and take her away to some place more interesting and exciting. Almost as soon as she wished it, she heard a cheerful voice behind her. "Prissy! There you are. I thought you would be here. How would you like to come with me on a Saturday carriage ride?"

Prissy looked up. "Miss Jane!" she cried, running to hug her. "Oh, I'm so glad you came! It's been dreadfully boring here. Can I really come with you?"

"Of course," said Miss Jane. "I'm going to see my Aunt Ellen. She invited me to her house yesterday. She sounded rather excited, and I'm curious to see what's up. Come along, now. We mustn't be late."

Prissy excitedly grabbed her bonnet and hurried after Miss Jane. It was a wonderful carriage drive, and Prissy enjoyed it immensely. The sun was shining brightly, the birds were chirping cheerfully, and the trees were dancing gaily in the warm summer breeze. Her gloomy day had suddenly turned into the most perfect day ever. Prissy looked at Miss Jane. Everything seemed more cheerful around Miss Jane. Her bubbly joy always poured out to others and cheered them up. It had certainly cheered Prissy up!

Before long, the carriage drew up in front of a small, pretty house. Beautiful green ivy grew on its sides, and just in front of the house, roses bloomed out of the dark, moist soil. It was a dear little house, and the outward appearance looked warm and welcoming, as if calling to passersby to come inside.

Miss Jane dropped the reins and got out of the buggy. Prissy decided to remain in the garden until Miss Jane was finished visiting with her aunt.

Miss Jane walked to the door and knocked on it with the knocker. A woman with white hair and a pretty, although frazzled-looking face opened the door. "Why Jane, aren't I glad to see you!" she cried, giving Miss Jane sloppy kisses on her cheek.

Miss Jane hugged her back. "Is everything all right, Aunt Ellen?" she asked. "You look rather out of sorts."

"Indeed I am. Please come inside, and I'll tell you everything."

Miss Jane stepped inside. The walls of Aunt Ellen's home were painted soft gold, which contrasted pleasantly with the royal red curtains that hung by the windows. It was finely furnished, with chairs and elegant furniture in the living room and cabinets containing expensive chinaware in the dining room. There were pictures of Aunt Ellen when she was young hanging above the mantelpiece. Miss Jane looked at them with interest. One picture was of an eight-year-old Ellen standing in her rose garden, her thick black hair pulled back into two braids. Her face was filled with happiness and the fullness of youth. She was a fair little maiden, with black, beady eyes that were filled with fun and mischief.

Aunt Ellen invited Miss Jane into her drawing-room. Miss Jane sat on a white chair trimmed with golden beads while Aunt Ellen chose a chair colored in a pretty pastel green with flowers carved into the wooden frame.

Miss Jane smiled at her aunt, whom she loved dearly. Aunt Ellen had looked after Miss Jane after her parents had passed away when she was a young girl. The schoolteacher had grown up under her care and was very close to her and Aunt Ellen's own daughter, Evelyn, who was currently attending college in New York.

"Now," Miss Jane said to Aunt Ellen, "tell me what's on your mind."

"Well," started Aunt Ellen, "it all began last Saturday when I accompanied my friend, Esther Hopkins, to the Hope Orphanage not far from here, where she was to pick up a little girl for herself. While I was there, I took a liking to a girl named Claire Barson, who reminded me a little of my dear older sister, Josie."

"Claire is only twelve years old. Her mother passed away when she was an infant, and Claire believes her father is in the army...but the truth is, nobody knows what's happened to him. Claire's spent all of her life moving from orphanage to orphanage, poor thing. Since she has no relatives anyone knows of, I decided to take her in last Saturday. But I'm not as lively as I used to be. It's certainly been some time since I was running around tending to you and Evelyn, though it feels like it was only yesterday! I didn't realize how challenging looking after a child would be, especially someone like Claire who has such an active imagination. And I don't think an old woman like me could do her the good she deserves!"

Miss Jane kissed Aunt Ellen's wrinkled face gently. "My dear aunt," she said, "I think you are doing a marvelous job. I know of no one who could do a better job loving someone than you!"

"Oh, Jane, you are sweet...but the reason I wanted you to swing by is because I've recently had the most glorious idea," Aunt Ellen said, grabbing Miss Jane's hand with sudden excitement. "I think *you're* just the young, kind, motherly soul Claire needs to look after her!"

"Oh, Aunt Ellen!" Miss Jane said, her aunt's outburst leaving her at a loss for words. "I really don't know if..."

"You're a marvel with children, you've got the kindest heart, and you're young with a load of energy still in you," Aunt Ellen interrupted. "You're perfect for Claire! And she's such a dear, I know you'll love her."

Aunt Ellen looked at Miss Jane with eyes so hopeful, the schoolteacher did not wish to disappoint her.

"You really are too kind to me, Aunt Ellen," Miss Jane said. "But I'm afraid I'm not as confident as you are in my ability to give Claire everything she needs..."

"She just needs someone who'll love her unconditionally and value her for the person she is...along with having that load of energy I was speaking about," Aunt Ellen quickly added.

Miss Jane smiled. "Well, if you're sure I could do her any good..."

"Marvelous!" Aunt Ellen cried, causing Miss Jane to jump slightly. "I knew you'd comply! Let me call Claire right now. Claire, Claire! Come down, please. There's someone who wants to meet you!"

The sound of footsteps on the stairs leading to the upstairs compartment of Aunt Ellen's home echoed in the living room. Before long, Claire was standing in front of them.

She was a tall, slim girl, with brown eyes and brown hair that was tied back tightly into two braids. Her face carried a rather solemn, opinionated-looking expression, and her nose was sharp. There was something about her twinkling brown eyes that made Miss Jane like her at once.

"How do you do," Claire said politely to the schoolteacher.

"Claire, this is Miss Jane," said Aunt Ellen. "She's my little girl! Well, she *was* a little girl when I took her in after her parents passed...and my little girl she'll always be!"

"I was around your age when Aunt Ellen took me in," Miss Jane said to Claire, giving her a kind smile.

"And now, she's grown into a lovely, wonderful woman," Aunt Ellen said, her face beaming. "Claire, dear, Miss Jane is the schoolteacher here. She lives right next door to the school in town. We were talking about the possibility of you going to live with her. You see, Miss Jane said she'd be very happy to take you in, and you'd easily be able to attend school, learn, and play with other kids your age. I'll come visit you often, of course. Would you like that?"

Claire observed Miss Jane. "I think so," she said, in a slow, thoughtful way. "Miss Jane seems like a nice person. Not like a lady who whips children when they misbehave. I usually get along well with those people."

"Claire!" exclaimed Aunt Ellen, shocked at Claire's outspoken manner. "My child, you must learn to keep certain thoughts to yourself and not say everything out loud."

"But I didn't say anything bad, did I?" said Claire, her eyes looking a little hurt. "I was just thinking about how I would describe Miss Jane in a book. A lady with kind, soft brown eyes, a charming smile, and an expression that appears to convey a relatively good temper. She appears to be perfect in every way, and I, a plain girl with humble origins, feel privileged to be in her presence, for she is…"

"Err…that's very nice, Claire," Aunt Ellen interrupted as a pink-faced Miss Jane giggled. "Come along upstairs, now. I'll help you pack all your things."

Aunt Ellen and Claire went upstairs to pack Claire's things while Miss Jane waited for them in the drawing-room. It was only about ten minutes before they returned.

"Well, Claire bear, you be good now, and don't give Miss Jane any trouble," Aunt Ellen said with a chirpy laugh as she embraced the younger girl. "I'll come see you next Saturday."

"Good-bye, Aunt Ellen," Claire said, hanging onto the older woman tightly. She had not received much affection during her lonely life as an orphan and yearned deeply for love. "I'll be waiting for you on Saturday."

Aunt Ellen gave Claire a departing kiss and a light pinch on her cheek. Then, Claire took Miss Jane's hand as she and the schoolteacher made their way out the house and toward the carriage.

Outside, Prissy was surprised to see Claire with Miss Jane. "Who's this?" she asked the schoolteacher as Claire climbed into the carriage next to her. Miss Jane told her, and Prissy was absolutely delighted at the thought of having Claire as a friend.

"I've never actually had a friend before," Claire informed Prissy. "You see, the children at the orphanage all thought I was a little strange, so they kept their distance."

"Why did they think you were strange?" Prissy asked curiously.

"Well, I used to scribble down little stories about all of them in a notebook I kept," Claire explained. "I imagined them all as wonderful, strong, courageous characters who all had better, happier lives and families that loved them immensely. One day, they found my book, and they laughed at my stories. They made fun of what I wrote because they didn't believe any of the stories could come true. I guess there's nothing wrong in being realistic, but I was offended with them and lost my temper. They had no right to insult my writing after I had worked so hard to make good characters out of them. No one really wanted anything to do with me after I blew my top like how I did. I can't really blame them because it isn't really their fault if they couldn't understand me. And I got used pretty quickly to being alone, anyway."

Miss Jane noticed that Claire's small face carried a pained look, and she felt a pang in her heart.

"I would love to read your stories, if you'll let me," the schoolteacher said gently. "I'm sure they're magnificent."

Claire's face brightened considerably. "Oh, I shall show you all of them, then! I've written one about my father, whom no one knows anything about. I think he's a brave soldier. He's currently fighting a war in Africa, and he's made alliances with the tribes there…"

Claire stopped and sighed. "I hope it's true. But I don't think anyone reading such a story would believe it, even if I do."

Claire turned to look at Miss Jane, her face filled with eagerness. "One day, I'm going to write a wonderful, beautiful story. A story that *is* true. A story that will touch people's hearts and make a difference."

Claire contentedly leaned back in her seat, her eyes thoughtful. "And when I write that story, I won't mind so much whether or not people choose to believe it. Because I'll believe in it. It'll be *my* story."

****

Claire was a sweet lass, and she blossomed under Miss Jane's care. She made many friends at school, who were rather taken with her creative imagination and the outspoken way she always spoke what she thought. Miss Jane loved her dearly and thought the world of her. But after coming to live with the schoolteacher, Claire's mischievous side soon shone through, and she got into many scrapes, some of which were serious, some rather funny, and some quite embarrassing.

There was one scrape in particular that Claire got into from which she learned a very important lesson—that dishonesty and disobedience only lead to trouble. It wasn't very funny when it happened, but years later, Miss Jane and Claire laughed about it together.

Miss Jane was a very fine artist. She had painted many illustrations for books, poems, and things of that sort. What with teaching and painting, Miss Jane was very busy.

One day, Miss Jane spent practically the entire morning painting. She worked and worked until she ran out of white paint. "Oh, bother!" she thought. "I shall have to go into town to get some more." With a sigh, she wrapped a shawl around her shoulders and trudged toward the front door. Miss Jane was very grumpy. Working hard for so long always made her so, and the fact that she had to stop for a while only irritated her more.

"Please don't go into the library," Miss Jane told Claire before she left. "All my paintings are in there and are still drying, and I don't want anything to mess them up. I'm going into town to get some more paint. I'll be back soon."

"Yes, Miss Jane," said Claire. Miss Jane walked out into the cold air, leaving Claire to her book.

Claire read her book till she had finished it. Then, she began looking for something else to do. But she found nothing to occupy her mind with, and she started getting very bored. "If only I had another book to read," she thought. She remembered that Miss Jane had told her not to go into the library. "I'll just go in quickly and get another one," thought Claire. "Besides, I have nothing to do. I won't mess anything up, and Miss Jane won't know anything."

Claire made her way to the library. Inside, there stood a painting of a handsome Great Dane. It looked so real that Claire's heart skipped a beat. Miss Jane had set it leaning against the desk to dry. The bookshelf was on the other side, so Claire carefully slid past the painting to get her book. She held her breath as she went across, and she was greatly relieved that nothing bad happened. Claire looked at all the books. The one she wanted was on the top shelf, a little above Claire's reach. Claire stood on her tiptoes to get it. She managed to push it a little with her forefinger, and then an awful thing happened. The book came crashing down, right on top of Claire's head! Alarmed, Claire jumped backward, knocking the painting to the floor.

Claire stood thunderstruck for several minutes. Frightening thoughts rushed through her mind all at once. Miss Jane would be so mad! Would she be punished badly? All of Claire's thoughts concerned herself. But then, one thought flashed through her mind that made her heart sink. Miss Jane had worked so hard, and she, Claire Barson, had ruined everything.

Claire picked up the painting gently, trembling like a leaf. The paint had not been dripping wet, thank goodness, but the damage was still done. Although the outline of the dog was still present, its once handsome features were nothing but smudges.

"Maybe Miss Jane will be able to fix it," thought Claire. Then, Claire had another thought, one that for many days after, she wished she had never had. "Maybe I can fix it! Then Miss Jane won't be mad, and nobody will know anything."

Before she knew it, Claire had taken a brush and cans of paint and was working on the ruined dog. Finally, she stood back, looked at the dog, and said, "Well, that's the best I can do. Hopefully, Miss Jane won't notice anything." And with that, she took her book and went into the drawing-room.

****

Miss Jane came home carrying a can of white paint. The fresh air had relaxed her nerves, and she felt less grumpy than before. Inside the house, she saw Claire reading quietly. Assuming that Claire had obeyed her orders, she went into the library. When she got there, she gasped and clutched the table in fright. There before her stood a most atrocious looking mongrel! It's once handsome, clear brown eyes were now just black blots, framed with what looked like girlish eyelashes. Its delicate ears that had perked up so realistically were now straight and pointed at the top like an elf's. Its snub nose was as long as a carrot. And the teeth! Oh, the horrible teeth! They were painted crookedly into a wide smile. The bad painter, realizing the lack of white paint, had used yellow instead, so the crooked teeth looked like they were decaying and falling out. The dog's once muscular legs were straight and skinny like a skeleton's. The hair on its body now all stood up like little brown sprouts of grass growing in the light of the sun. Its feet were now round brown circles that had long, thorn-like nails growing from them.

Miss Jane trembled, and her face filled with dismay. Her dog! Her beautiful dog which she had worked so hard on was ruined! The shock had quite taken her breath away. But now that she was beginning to recover, she felt a sense of extreme disappointment. She had worked so hard on her painting. There was no way she could fix it now. She would have to do it all over again, and that would take her forever.

"Claire! Come here!" she cried. She knew that Claire had done this. Who else could have? Claire came into the library, looking most innocent.

"Yes, Miss Jane?" she asked in a sweet voice, trying to keep it from shaking.

Miss Jane had learned by now that the more innocent Claire looked, the guiltier she was. "Claire, did you do this?"

"Well, yes, Miss Jane. I'm extremely sorry. I didn't mean to mess it up. I came here to get a book, and I toppled the

"Claire, did you do this?"

painting over. I tried to fix it, but I guess it isn't very good."

Miss Jane sighed. "Claire, that painting cost me a lot of time and energy, and now I have to start all over. The fact that you disobeyed me hurts me much more than the painting. I'm afraid I'm very disappointed. Please go to your room and think about what you've done. I need some time to think about all this."

Claire felt very sad and upset. Miss Jane's words and her disappointed face had gone to her heart like a dagger. She slowly dragged her feet up the stairs and went into her room.

Miss Jane sighed and plopped down into a chair. She looked at the painting, feeling miserable. But when she saw the girlish eyelashes and the wide yellow smile, the funny side of the incident hit her, and she laughed till tears poured down her cheeks. Feeling better, she made her way to Claire's room, ready to give her one more chance.

****

When Miss Jane came into Claire's room, she found Claire lying on her bed, sobbing into her pillow. Miss Jane went to her and stroked her hair. Claire got up, her tear-stained face looking at Miss Jane. "Miss Jane," she said, "I really am sorry. I didn't mean to ruin everything! I'm so sorry for being disobedient. Please forgive me!"

"I forgive you, Claire," said Miss Jane. "But you must know that once you do something wrong, you should always confess. It is never a good idea to try to hide your sin."

"It is so hard to be honest from the beginning though, isn't it?"

"Yes, it is," Miss Jane agreed. "But hiding sin just makes a bigger mess of things. If you had told me right away that you had ruined the painting instead of trying to hide the damage, I might have been able to fix it with less trouble. But now, since you've tried to cover up your mistakes, it will take much more time and energy to work through all the extra amount of paint to bring out what is good and true underneath."

Claire nodded thoughtfully. "I see what you're saying," she said, her creative thinking coming into play. "If we confess our sin to God instead of trying to cover it up, He'll remove our sin from us and renew us. But if we try to cover up our sin, we'll have to go through so much more pain than we would if we had confessed at the beginning. We should always bring our mess to the one true artist who alone can bring out what is true and pure underneath."

Miss Jane nodded. "I think, Claire," she said with a smile, "that you've just about got it right."

Chapter Four: The Helping Hands Club is Formed

"Do not neglect to do good and to share what you have, for such sacrifices are pleasing to God." Hebrews 13:16

A group of five children sat on the school lawn one bright, sunny day. All of them wore their best clothes, and it was obvious that they were holding a very important meeting. Abel sat at the front, wearing his Sunday best suit, complete with a handkerchief popping out from his jacket pocket, just like grownups. He wore his dad's polished shoes, which were much too big for him (and it must be confessed that he took these without his dad knowing). He sat up straight and had the commanding air of a leader. He had to, of course, since he was elected as the president of the club.

Next came Pat, who, despite his great position as vice president, just couldn't look solemn. Instead, he was all smiles on this pleasant day. He also looked rather smart. For once, he had taken the pains to comb his red hair, but nothing would make him wash his face, making it obvious to all the other children that he had had eggs for breakfast. He had on his least dirty trousers and a nice striped, red shirt. His mother wouldn't allow him to wear his suit, afraid that he would get it all dirty. He had red shoes on his feet that looked nice and clean.

Next in command were Charlie and Prissy, who were the cabinet. Charlie cared nothing for looking important and wore his plain everyday clothes. He wore no shoes and was presently trying to catch a lizard that was coming out of Pat's pocket. Prissy sat next to him. She was just the opposite of Mr. Charles Thompson. She wore a pretty pink frock and a pair of pearl-white sandals. Her golden hair curled like Goldilocks', and she wore a white bow at the back of her head. Her small dainty hands folded in her lap, and her face carried a patient look, the look of one containing great wisdom. She had practiced making faces in the mirror to see which one was the most dignified. She had at last found the right one and felt like it was a great success.

Next was Claire. She wore a plain, pleated frock, and her brown eyes sparkled with fun and eagerness. She had on her everyday black boots, and on her nose sat a pair of glasses which were atrociously big and fake. She thought that wearing them would make her look more like an editor and writer. Everyone knew that Claire had a great gift of writing, and no easier choice could have been made as to who should be the editor and writer of the group.

Abel waited until everyone was fairly settled and then began the speech he had prepared.

"We have gathered here on the fourth of March to discuss the conditions and responsibilities that come with being a member of this group. He that does not—" Abel stopped and looked sternly at Charlie, who was struggling to hold the squirming lizard.

"Mr. Thompson, do you wish a demotion from position?"

"No, Mr. President. No, indeed," said Charlie, trying to sit on the squirming animal.

"That's my lizard!" cried Pat furiously. "Don't sit on him!"

"So the lizard is yours?" asked Abel.

"Ye—ye—yes, Mr. President," stuttered Pat. "He must have escaped when I wasn't looking."

"Then I kindly ask that from here on you make sure he *stays* in your pocket, and that he does not *leave* your pocket. Do you understand?"

"Yes," Pat replied, shoving the lizard into his pocket.

"Well, anyway," continued Abel, "as I was saying, he that does not wish to be a member of this club must say so now, or forever hold his peace."

He stopped and waited for a response from anyone who wished to resign from the club, but as no one said anything, he continued. "We have formed this club to help others in the world. Each member will strive to help someone every day, and at the end of the week, we'll all meet together here in the schoolyard to discuss what we have done. We'll also try to come up with solutions to any problems we may have come across. Miss Barson, will you please rise and read us the requirements of being a member of this club?"

"Yes, Abel...I mean, Mr. President," said Claire, rising to her feet. She turned around and faced the expectant faces looking at her. She pulled out a crumpled piece of paper from her pocket and, pushing her glasses closer to her eyes, she began to read.

"Ladies and gentlemen—I am so glad that we have been able to come together on the fourth of March to form a club that is good and beneficial for the community. Here are the expectations that each member must live up to. If any member wishes to dispute any of these laws, he must speak to the president and vice president after the meeting, and if the president agrees, the law in question will be declared null. Let us begin:

Helping Hands - Bylaws for Members:

1. This club is henceforth called 'Helping Hands,' to honor the recommendation of the vice president.
2. This club is formed to show the love of Jesus by helping others in need.
3. There will be no competition between members as to who does the most important work.
4. No human will reward members for the work they do. The reward for each members' loving actions will be given by the almighty Father who dwells in heaven, in His own good time.

5. If a member exhibits haughtiness or pettiness of any form, there will be an automatic demotion from position.
6. If a member finds nothing nice to do during the week, he must give a clear and truthful explanation. If the member did nothing nice just because he didn't want to, he will face certain consequences.
7. No member should hide anything from the rest of the club. Additionally, matters discussed confidentially between members are not to be discussed with anyone else.
8. There should be no dishonesty of any kind.
9. Members' actions should always be kind.
10. Members should please God in everything they do and say.

Members must hereby rise and promise to carry out their duties. Each member is responsible to God for all the things he does."

Here, Prissy, Charlie, and Pat rose and solemnly promised to be truthful and to do everything that was required of them.

Then, Claire continued reading:

"The Helping Hands - Bylaws for President:

1. The President should always ask God for advice when confronted with a problem.
2. The President should be a good example for the rest of the members.
3. The President should always be ready to listen to each member's problems properly and respectfully.
4. If the President does something wrong or frightening that affects the members terribly, he will be demoted, and the vice president will take his place.
5. The President can stay in office for 3 months, and then he will give up his position to one who has earned respect and proved dependable.

6. The President must not be too bossy and push his weight around.
7. The President must be in agreement with the vice president when he passes a law.
8. The President must share in all the work that the members do.
9. The President must be considerate of the members' feelings at all times.
10. The President is accountable for all that he does and says.

"The President must hereby rise and promise to carry out his duties. He is responsible to God for all the things he does."

Abel rose and promised as the members had done. Then, Claire put her right hand on her heart and, holding her left hand in the air, promised to do everything required to be a member of the committee. She also said, "I, Claire Barson, promise as writer and editor of this group, not to write any falsehoods in our local paper."

"Good, good," said Abel. "Now, we must hand out the daily record sheets. Mr. Vice President, will you please pass them out?"

"Certainly," said Pat. Walking around with a stack of papers, he gave each member one of the sheets that had been prepared by him and Abel.

The members bent their heads and studied the paper. Here is what it looked like:

Monday	Tuesday	Wednesday	Thursday	Friday

Each day of the week, each member would have to do three nice things. Then, at the end of each day, they would list the three things they had done on their record sheets. Each

Saturday, they would meet on the school lawn for their weekly meeting and discuss how their helping hands had helped others.

Abel explained all this as best as he could and passed out a legal document, asking for the members to sign their names. This made certain that each person legally belonged to the club. The document ran thus:

This is to certify that each person has promised to be committed to the Helping Hands club.

Signed:

Abel Blackstone	Pat Hooky
President	*Vice President.*
Charlie T.	Priscilla Diane Robinson
Cabinet	*Cabinet*
Claire M. Barson	
ED/W	

After they had all signed their names, Pat gave the paper to Abel. After a few more words, the meeting was over, and everyone was dismissed. The "grownups" were done for the day, and they all became children again, going to Prissy's house for a snack of milk and cookies, prepared by the jolly cook. Each member was determined to do something nice for someone in the week that followed.

Chapter Five: A Soft Answer Turns Away Wrath

"A soft answer turns away wrath, but a harsh word stirs up anger." Proverbs 15:1

Monday came, sunny and without a cloud in the blue sky. Prissy jumped out of bed and drew the curtains back. The sun streamed into the room, bringing joy and happiness with it. Prissy washed her rosy face and combed her silky, golden locks. She was in a special mood today, so she put on her sunny yellow frock, pinned on a golden brooch, and slid her feet into pretty white sandals. She opened her dresser drawer, taking out the Helping Hands record sheet. "I have to do three nice things today," she said to her reflection in the mirror. "Now, what nice thing should I do first?"

She walked down the stairs, pondering, when the Robinsons' grumpy maid, Eliza, waved a dirty duster in her face. Prissy jumped back as the specks of dust flew onto her face and frock. Horrified, she brushed them away, coughing all the while. "I've had enough of you!" cried Eliza, her sharp hazel eyes boring into Prissy. "Each day, I clean this horrible mansion, only to have it dirtied again. You are an inconsiderate, selfish little doll! Look at you, sliding your dirty hand against my clean banister! You are a messy, horrible little princess, and I'm sick and tired of you!"

Prissy looked at her hands, which were actually very clean and white. She stared at Eliza, preparing to say something really bad. Instead, she bit her lip. Wasn't this the first opportunity to be kind to someone? Wouldn't Jesus be nice to the people who were mean to him? Prissy choked back her mean words, the effort almost killing her. With much trouble, she said in a soft, gentle voice, "I'm dreadfully sorry, Eliza. I didn't realize how much trouble it took you to clean the house. I'll be more careful from here on not to get things dirty and to pick up after myself. Maybe, after I come home from school, I could help you tidy up?"

Eliza straightened, surprised at Prissy's calm, respectful answer. Her eyes became softer, and the crease on her forehead lessened. She spoke in an unusually soft voice. "Sure. Just be more careful next time. I guess I was a little too hard."

Prissy gazed in amazement. She suddenly realized that Eliza might have a kind soul under all her grumpiness. And to think it took her so long to find out!

"Have a good day," she said as she went into the kitchen. She had learned an important lesson—that a soft answer turns away anger. She felt very pleased. She had overcome her anger, and today, she was going to use her helping hands to help Eliza clean!

Chapter Six: Giving to the Lord

"Whoever is generous to the poor lends to the Lord, and he will repay him for his deed." Proverbs 19:17

It was "Special Sandwich Day" over at the Thompson's house. Charlie's mom made the best sandwiches, and each Monday, she made a sandwich filled with lettuce, bacon and tomatoes and topped with melted cheese for Charlie and his dad. It was one of Charlie's favorites, which automatically made Monday his favorite day of the week. He watched eagerly, his stomach growling, as his mom made his sandwich with delicate fingers. She put it in his lunch pail and handed it to him.

"Now, shoo! Go to school!" the jolly, plump woman said. "And mind you don't eat your meal on the way!"

"Yes, Ma," Charlie said, going out the front door. "Will you make something nice for dinner? And make lots of it, so I can have more than just two helpings."

"Oh, you naughty boy!" said Mrs. Thompson, laughing.

Charlie walked on the dirt road, sniffing inside his lunch pail. The sweet aroma circled beneath his nostrils, and his mouth watered. The only bad thing about Mondays was that his ma always made him promise not to eat his meal before lunchtime. Oh, it was complete agony! Charlie's stomach growled, and his fingers itched to hold the delicious sandwich.

Charlie tightly gripped his lunch pail

Charlie looked at the birds to take his mind off his lunch. As he looked, he saw one bird peck a worm from the ground and give it to another bird. Suddenly, he remembered. "Why, today's the first day of the week!" he said to himself. "I have to help people. It's a good thing that bird reminded me. It would have been awful if I broke all my solemn vows. Hey, thanks birdie!"

Charlie shook his head as he thought of how he could have forgotten. In truth, he frequently forgot things. The only thing he never forgot, was when it was time to eat, which was most unfortunate for him!

Charlie had not walked far when he saw a boy sitting at the corner of the road. His clothes were torn, and he looked very poor. He looked weak and hungry. "Poor fellow," said Charlie. "I wish I could help him." It took some time before it dawned on him. "I can help him!" Charlie thought. "I can give him my food!"

But that was too much for Charlie, and the thought cut his heart like a dagger. Part with his lovely sandwich? The one he had been waiting all week for? Never! Charlie tightly gripped his lunch pail. He tried to ignore the inner voice speaking in his heart, but he couldn't. "You should give it to him," it kept saying. "Isn't that what Jesus would do? Charlie, He gave His *life* for you, and you won't give someone food?

"But it's not the same," argued Charlie. "It's not like I'm giving *Jesus* my food!"

"Oh, yes it is," said the voice. "Remember what Miss Jane taught you and your class last week? She said that giving to the poor is giving to the Lord. It says so in Proverbs 19:17. It also says that if you give to the poor, the Lord will repay you for your deed."

Charlie looked at his lunch. He remembered how the bird had given the other bird his food. Couldn't he do the same? After all, he was giving to Jesus, and it was nothing compared to what Jesus had given him. So, Charlie went and gave the boy his lunch, and he walked away with something far greater than food that day!

Chapter Seven: Loving Your Enemy

"But I say to you who hear, Love your enemies, do good to those who hate you." Luke 6:27

Abel walked into town in the sweltering heat. Many people looked his way, for Abel was not a person who went easily unnoticed. Many observed that he was a tall and solid-looking boy. He had dark brown hair and tanned skin, and his eyes, brown and clear, were filled with thoughtfulness and quiet dignity. He took long strides as he walked, and he held his head up high.

Anybody could tell that he was a boy with plenty of courage and honor. Abel hardly told any lies, considering them shameful and cowardly. Indeed, he had his standards.

Abel had not always been this way. He used to get into plenty of fights with the boys in his old town, who called themselves The Big Bang. Abel was not a person to take a seat or be trampled on, but as Miss Jane had told him, "Being bold and standing up for what you believe doesn't mean you have to tread on someone else's toes."

Lies and deceit had never been Abel's weakness, but fighting had. His days in Miss Jane's school had been filled with learning to forgive and love others.

Abel had learned these lessons willingly, and on this day, it was time for him to take his first test.

Going into the department store, Abel saw Pat buying a toy for a younger child.

"Hey, Pat," he said, going over to him.

Pat looked up. "Hi, Abel!" he said, his green eyes twinkling. "Looks like you caught me in the act of helping someone!"

Abel smiled. "You are definitely doing a good job. Have you managed to find three nice things to do a day?" asked Abel.

"Oh yes. There are plenty of ways to help. Too bad it took me all this time to realize it," replied Pat.

"Yeah, I've realized that people want to know more about Jesus when they see his followers doing nice things. I'm afraid Christians speak a lot but don't act," sighed Abel.

"Yep, you're right. I'm just about done here. Can I help you do your shopping?" asked Pat.

"Nah, it's okay, I can manage."

Pat looked at him pleadingly. "Please, Abel?" he said. "If you let me help you, I can add it to my record sheet."

Abel grinned. "You sly fox! Well, thanks, I guess I can use the help. Miss Jane needs me to buy her two bags of flour."

"The flour's right over there, see? C'mon, I'll help you carry the bags!"

After Pat was done helping Abel with his shopping, they both left the store and went outside.

There, they saw a boy with a rather embarrassed face picking up items that had fallen out of his basket. The things he had bought were continually being trampled by carriages and busy people. No one was helping him pick up his things.

Abel looked at him. He recognized him as one of the boys from The Big Bang. Abel grinned. Those boys had mistreated him many times, and it felt good to see one of them getting what they deserved. Then, while he was still crowing over the boy's trials, the class verse which Miss Jane had helped them memorize came to his mind. *"But I say to you which hear, Love your enemies, do good to those who hate you."*

Abel grimaced. He didn't really want to help someone who had always been mean to him. But since he was a Christian, shouldn't he show the love of Christ even to those who were his enemies? After all, wasn't the Helping Hands club formed to help others whether or not they deserved it?

Abel sighed. He knew what the right thing to do was. It was just so hard. "Oh Lord," he prayed. "Pour your love in my heart so I can share it with this boy!" Abel walked toward the boy and knelt down beside him. He started picking up the items. "Hi," he said. "I thought you might need some help. You know, it's rather hard not to drop anything when you're carrying so much."

The boy looked at Abel with a surprised and grateful face. "Thanks a lot," he said. "You're nice." Abel looked at him and smiled. Before long, he was sharing the gospel with the boy, helped along by Pat.

When Abel and Pat were walking back together, Pat looked at Abel thoughtfully. "That was very nice of you, Abel," he said. "Being nice to one of the Big Bang boys is not easy. You were doing good to those that do evil, and look what happened? That boy accepted Christ as his Savior."

"Yeah," said Abel, grinning. "It was marvelous, wasn't it? I'm glad I allowed God to show His love through me!"

Chapter Eight: The Greatest Helping Hands

"For I the Lord your God will hold your right hand; it is I who say to you Fear not, I am the one who helps you." Isaiah 41:13

Claire was sitting in the living room reading a Shakespeare book when Miss Jane came rushing in through the front door. She quickly closed the door and hurried to Claire.

"Claire," she said in a shaky voice, "aunt Ellen is very ill."

Claire dropped her book and jumped up immediately. Miss Jane's face was filled with worry and stress.

"Is she very bad?" Claire asked.

"I'm afraid so," replied Miss Jane.

Aunt Ellen was very dear to Miss Jane. Besides being like a mother to her after her parents had passed away, Aunt Ellen was the one who had led Miss Jane to Jesus, and Miss Jane loved her very much.

Claire loved Aunt Ellen very much as well. Why, they did everything together. They went on picnics, and they sat together in church. Claire hadn't had much love in her life. Her mother had died as soon as she was born, and her father...well, nobody really knew anything about him. As a result, Claire immediately grew close to anyone who showed her love and kindness.

"I'm going into town for the doctor," Miss Jane said. "I'm going to stay with Aunt Ellen and look after her until she is better. I'll leave you at Prissy's house. Her parents are in town, and Mrs. Robinson said that she would be happy to have you."

Claire didn't want to be left behind. "Miss Jane, is there anything I can do to help Aunt Ellen?"

"I'm afraid not," Miss Jane said. "All we can do is pray."

Claire was not used to just praying without doing anything. She was a strong-willed girl who bustled here and there, always doing things for people; but she didn't like just sitting still and praying silently for someone. She had never thought that would do much good.

"Miss Jane, please let me come with you," Claire pleaded. "I can help you. You can't do everything on your own. It would exhaust you. I can do plenty of things! And besides, I enjoy nursing."

Miss Jane looked doubtful, but finally gave her consent after Claire's pleading. So, Claire, thoroughly satisfied at having her way, quickly packed her things and left with Miss Jane for Aunt Ellen's house.

The doctor came and confirmed that Aunt Ellen had scarlet fever and was very ill. He wasn't pleased that Claire was in Aunt Ellen's house, because he feared she would get ill as well. But Claire had already had scarlet fever when she was five, and Miss Jane had had it when she was fifteen. The doctor prescribed the medicine and left.

Miss Jane and Claire worked very hard to care for Aunt Ellen. Miss Jane stayed up all night, giving Aunt Ellen her medicine when she needed it, and Claire ran here and there, getting water or anything that made Aunt Ellen or Miss Jane comfortable.

But slowly, Aunt Ellen grew worse. She began to have coughing fits and became too weak to even sit up. Since Claire couldn't be of much help, she was sent to stay with Prissy. The school had to hire a substitute teacher since Miss Jane couldn't leave Aunt Ellen's bedside.

One day, when Claire was at Prissy's house, news came that Aunt Ellen might never pull through. Claire was stunned and went alone to her bedroom. Prissy followed her.

"Claire," Prissy called softly. "Are you all right?"

Claire looked at her. "Prissy, I feel so helpless. Miss Jane sent me away because there was nothing I could do. But there must be something. There has to be!" she cried.

Prissy sat beside her on the bed and took her hand. "Claire," she said. "There's still something you can do. You can pray."

"Oh, Prissy!" Claire jumped up. "I have already prayed. But I feel that's not enough. I have to do something."

But Prissy didn't agree. "Claire," she said gently. "Ever since we formed the Helping Hands club, I've felt that we've forgotten to make something clear. I've kept my mouth shut about it, but I'm going to tell you now.

"Claire, we can use our hands to help others, and we should. It's right to help others. But sometimes, we come to a point in our lives where our hands are not capable of doing what is needed. We cannot make someone well, as you already know. Some things are just impossible for us to do. During these times, we should take our problem to the Helping Hands that made you and me—to the One who holds the world in the palm of His hand. We should take our problems and place them in God's hands, for nothing is impossible for Him. Don't you see?"

"Yes, I do," said Claire, nodding her head. "Thanks, Prissy. God's hands are the greatest Helping Hands. I should take my problem to Him. Will you pray with me?"

"Sure," Prissy replied.

Both girls bowed their heads. "Lord, we know that our way is not always your way. It's my desire that you heal Aunt Ellen. I love her so very much. But I place my desires and worries in your hands, and I trust you," prayed Claire.

News later came to Claire and Prissy that Aunt Ellen had taken a turn for the better. Claire and Prissy were so happy, and they thanked God for healing her.

It was a week later, and the Helping Hands club was seated on the school lawn. Claire was standing up before them with a piece of paper in her hand.

"Friends," she said. "I have learned a very important lesson, and I want to share it with you. I've written a poem, and I'd like to read it to you."

She cleared her throat and began.

Helping Hands

Helping hands that help everywhere,
Helping hands that do a good deed,
Can show others that you really care,
And can bless someone that is in need.

Helping hands show the love that you feel,
Helping hands show compassion so true.
Helping hands can show that God's real,
When His will, with your helping hands, you do.

But when helping hands can do nothing,
And the situation is all in God's will,
What can helping hands be doing,
When God asks them to be still?

Your helping hands can fold together,
When for a person you do pray,
Your helping hands can go to God in prayer,
As that need, at God's feet, you lay.

When the situation is too big for your hands so little,
You can take it to Him who holds the earth in His palm,
For any big thing, God's hands can handle,
And can make any raging storm calm.

When our helping hands are so weak,
We can take it to the one who helps us along.
When you can't do a thing, those helping hands, you can seek,
Ours are weak, but His are strong.

The One whose hands made the heaven,
And also formed the sea,
Has in His hands graven,
The names of you and me.

So, whatever God calls your helping hands to do,
In His hands, you can find rest,
You can tell others that God is true,
For His glory, in you, will be manifest.

She finished, and there was a loud uproar of clapping. "That's beautiful, Claire," Prissy said. "I think that this poem should be the theme of the Helping Hands club. What do you say, everybody?"

Everybody agreed at once, and it has been the theme of the Helping Hands club from that day until now.

And so, Claire learned a very important lesson, one that is important for every child of God to learn—whenever a situation seems impossible to handle, just place it in God's hands, for His hands are the greatest Helping Hands.

Chapter Nine: Thankfulness

"Give thanks in all circumstances; for this is the will of God in Christ Jesus for you." 1 Thessalonians 5:18

It was a beautiful Monday morning, and all the students sat quietly in their seats, waiting patiently. They could tell that Miss Jane had something very important to say.

"Good morning, class," Miss Jane said, giving her students a warm smile. Her pretty face glowed with the fun idea she had thought of over the weekend, and the students felt an immense liking for her whenever her eyes twinkled like how they did now.

"Over the weekend, I had a brilliant idea, and I'm sure you all will like it. I got up Saturday morning and felt so happy as I saw the sunlight streaming into my little room. I realized that I was thankful for the sun—although sometimes, I've complained that it gives me a headache—and I just couldn't imagine what life would be without the sun."

The students stared at their teacher in bewilderment. They didn't see where she was going with her idea, talking about the sun and whatnot.

"I found to my surprise that I had never thanked God for the sun, and I did so right away," Miss Jane went on. "I suddenly realized that there were many things I took for granted, things that I forgot to be thankful for. Class, consider this question: if you only had today the things you were thankful for yesterday, would you have very much?"

The class looked at each other and pondered the question. There were some expert complainers and whiners in the class, and they looked at the floor guiltily.

Miss Jane continued her speech. "Class, God has given us so much, and many days go by when we forget to thank Him and choose to complain instead. I say we should all try our best to not let a day go by without counting our blessings and thanking our Provider, don't you? It's never too late to start, which is why I am giving you all this assignment. I want you all to write a paper by Friday about one specific thing that you are thankful for. Be as creative as you like! You can write an essay, a story, or even a poem. Just be sure to have it done on time so you can read it to the rest of the class. What do you say, students? Do you like my idea?"

"Yes, Miss Jane!" the class replied enthusiastically, eager to start on their project at once.

The students all took Miss Jane's advice to heart, and everyone was surprised to find how good it felt when you were thankful and content! Soon, Friday came, and every student had a paper to read about what he or she was thankful for.

First, it was Charlie's turn, and he stood in the front of the class, holding his paper in his hand. He hurriedly finished chewing the last bite of his chocolate bar and began to read what he had written.

"I am thankful for the food I have on my table, and for a wonderful ma who knows how to cook it well. Food is a necessary element of life, so you might as well enjoy it. I feel sad for people who go to bed with empty stomachs, and I am so grateful that I always go to bed with a full stomach—sometimes one that's a little *too* full. I know that if I ever run out of food, I would have eaten enough so far to keep me going. It would be dreadful not even to have had breakfast, and I can't imagine how it is to starve for days. So, that's what I'm thankful for. I'm thankful for a lot of other things, of course, but I would take up all of class time if I kept going, so you're just going to have to be satisfied and see me after class if you want any more information."

Charlie finished and looked at Miss Jane. "I'm finished," he said. "That's the best ending I could think of."

Miss Jane smiled. "That was wonderful, Charlie. We should all be grateful that we have something to eat every day, and I'm glad that you have taught us that simple lesson."

The class clapped, and Charlie went back to his seat, popping another chocolate into his mouth on the way.

Next was Pat's turn, and when he stood up, he was very red in the face. He read his paper, talking rapidly.

"I'm thankful for the many animals that God has made. It is wonderful to see how he has designed every creature in a unique way. I marvel at the frog, for instance, with its long tongue and four tiny legs that give it its ability to hop so high. I'm sure I would never have thought of creating such an animal. Looking at all these creatures lets me see how creative, clever, and wonderful our God is, and it makes me want to know Him even more. He exhibits His glory and magnificence through all of creation, and I'm grateful that He lets us behold His art each and every day."

"Very good, Pat!" Miss Jane said as the class clapped loudly. "Thank you for the lesson you have taught us. I'm sure most us don't thank God for his beautiful creation like we should."

Pat scampered off to his desk and sank into his seat gratefully. Speaking in front of others always made him nervous, although he didn't know why.

Prissy came after, and she beamed at the class as she read her essay. She had worked for hours on it and thought it quite good. She didn't care if anyone thought otherwise, for she was quite sure she could convince them they were wrong.

"I am thankful for the clothes I have to wear each day. I know it is a blessing to be dressed well and feel the warmth of my mittens and hood when it is bitterly cold. I know that sometimes I think too much about the things that I have, and my focus is often on the provision instead of the provider. I want to thank the Lord today for blessing me with clothes to wear. I'm grateful I have the option to choose how I want to dress when some people would give everything to have one simple outfit. I'm glad that God has given me so much, and I could never repay Him enough. But I'll give Him all the gratitude I've got in my heart."

"Well done, Prissy," Miss Jane said, giving the girl a smile. "It is often that we forget to be thankful for the clothes that we have to wear each day, and I'm glad that you have brought that to our attention."

Abel was after Prissy, and he strode to the front of the class, clearing his throat before he began.

"I am thankful to God for giving me a wonderful school where I can learn many new things. I've learned so much since I have been to Miss Jane's school, and I'm so glad that I was given the opportunity to learn about God and accept Him as my Savior. The school I go to is truly the best one around, for it teaches things that are more important than just Math and Science. It teaches about a Father who is kind and loving, unwilling for any of His children to perish. I am glad I came to this school, because it's here that I truly realized how wonderful Jesus is."

Miss Jane blinked back tears that involuntarily sprang to her eyes. She thought back to the old days when she was a much younger Miss Jane, with much less experience, trying so hard to start the school of her dreams. She had dreamt of a place where children of all ages would come to know their Father who would never forsake them and would always love them. She had clung to the hope and promise God had given her—that if she waited patiently on Him, He would pave the way and lead her to the purpose He had for her life. During those hard, long years, the Lord had taken Miss Jane to His School of Life, where she studied as a pupil until she was finally ready to begin the task which she was called to do. With all the experience the years had given her, Miss Jane had grown into a strong Christian, using the lessons she had learned to now teach young children, both poor and rich, weak and strong. She felt it was worth all the times she had felt tired and discouraged to now see children like Abel, transformed by the Lord into beautiful young men and women filled with the love of Christ and with a joy that surpasses anything worldly pleasures offer.

The class clapped, and Miss Jane patted Abel's shoulder. "That was wonderful, Abel," she said with a smile. "I, too, am grateful that you came to this school; it is children like you that make this school what it is."

Abel blushed, which was most unusual for him, and went back to his desk, feeling pleased. He did not like writing, but he had written his little essay from his heart, and he was glad that it had turned out all right.

Claire was next, and she stood in front of the class, excited to read the little poem which she had written. She had been thrilled with the project Miss Jane had assigned to the class, for she loved to write.

She began to read, and the class listened intently. This is what Claire's poem said:

The Captain at the Wheel

There was a ship not long ago,
Which was left abandoned onshore,
Its damaged stern, its battered bow,
Could be used no more.

Off its course, this ship was led,
Forced by a dreadsome gale,
Those who passed by on the beach always said,
"Never again will it sail."

It seemed the vessel so broken,
Was condemned to a terrible fate,
Never could it battle the ocean,
It was in such a dreadful state.

Then one day, the master carpenter came,
And repaired the ship like new,
And nothing was ever the same,

When the master, the ship, did rescue.

The vessel, no more, was empty,
For inside it, the captain did live,
Together they journeyed across the sea,
A new life, the captain did give.

Though many storms, the ship did fight,
And harshness, it did feel,
It always defeated its gruesome plight,
When the captain was at its wheel.

Like that ship, I was before,
Battered, defeated, and worn,
It seemed I could be used no more,
My sails were ripped and torn.

But the master to me came,
And made me whole again,
And nothing was the same,
When I made Him my captain.

Jesus, in me, does now dwell,
He cleansed me from within,
He took and made me a usable vessel,
And He removed from me all my sin.

Are you tired and distressed today?
Are your sails tattered and torn?
Do you not know the right way?
Are you defeated and very worn?

Friend, do not let yourself feel,
Discouraged and sad within,
Just let Jesus take over the wheel,
And cleanse you from your sin.

For when Christ is your captain,
A new life, you will be given,
You'll be made whole again,
And have a way to heaven.

I'm thankful for what God did for me,
When a new life, to me, He gave,
I'll praise my Savior thankfully,
For His mercy that does save.

I'm thankful I now am His,
Gratitude only I feel,
I'm so glad that my Savior now is,
Jesus, the captain at the wheel.

Claire finished and stopped for breath, while the rest of the class erupted into applause. They all loved poems and admired Claire's talent for being able to write them.

"Very good, Claire," Miss Jane said, smiling pleasantly. "I am very pleased with all of you. I'd say that you all did a marvelous job with this assignment, thanking God for things special to each one of us. Thankfulness is a powerful thing. It shines amid darkness, canceling out greed. With thankfulness, we find that even the small things of this life are things to praise our Heavenly Father for. Thankfulness turns selfishness into selflessness as we focus on the provider instead of the provisions. Always be thankful, dears, and remember that thankfulness is a blessing in and of itself."

Chapter Ten: Charlie's Talent

"As each has received a gift, use it to serve one another, as good stewards of God's varied grace: ¹¹ whoever speaks, as one who speaks oracles of God; whoever serves, as one who serves by the strength that God supplies—in order that in everything God may be glorified through Jesus Christ. To him belong glory and dominion forever and ever. Amen." 1 Peter 4:10-11

Everyone was excited. It was the last day of school before Christmas vacation! Christmas presents were exchanged between the students and close friends, and Miss Jane found her desk filled to the top with Christmas presents before the day was over.

"Class," said Miss Jane, "I am going to have a Christmas Eve dinner. Everyone is invited, along with his or her family and friends. You are free to bring any contribution to the meal or any dessert that you want. After dinner, we'll be going Christmas caroling, and you are welcome to take part in that if you would like. We'll go into town and give out some blankets, food, and Bibles to the needy and tell them the Good News. It will be a splendid night! What do you say?"

"Sounds great, Miss Jane," said Pat.

Claire raised her hand.

"Yes, Claire?" Miss Jane said.

"Abel, Pat, Charlie, Prissy and I are working on a Christmas pageant to perform sometime. Would it be possible for us to perform it during the Christmas Eve dinner?"

"Yes, of course. That's a great idea, Claire!"

More questions were asked about the dinner. Then, the students did a little Math and English and were dismissed early for their break.

"All right, everyone," Claire said to her friends as soon as they were out the door, "come on over to my house so we can discuss the pageant!"

The five children were soon in Claire's room, munching on chocolate cookies and discussing the pageant.

"Claire should write the script, of course," said Abel. "She loves writing, and she's the best at it. She'd do a fine job. I'll make the props. I'm good at carpentry."

"I'll sew the costumes," said Prissy.

"Will there be any barn animals involved?" asked Pat.

"Well, that would be cool," Claire said. "They couldn't come in the house, though. But I was thinking that we should just perform the pageant outside. There'll be more room that way."

"Good," said Pat. "I'll train the animals. I'm best at that!"

"What will you do, Charlie?" asked Prissy.

"I don't know," Charlie shrugged. "I'll just help and go with the flow."

The others looked at him but said nothing. They went back to talking about the play.

Everyone had something to do, and everyone was busy. Everyone, that is, except Charlie.

Charlie didn't mind at first, but it soon bothered him. He didn't want to be the only one not doing anything.

He went and spoke to Claire about it. "Claire," he said, "everybody is doing something for the pageant except me. Isn't there anything I could do?"

Claire bit her pencil and thought. "Well, Charlie, from what I've written so far, it seems like we don't have enough people for all the parts. I need someone who has a beautiful voice to sing. I need people who are great at acting to be Mary and Joseph. I need someone to be the angel and people to be the shepherds. We need to get barn animals, and I have no idea where to go. You can help with all of that if you like."

"I will," said Charlie, glad to be doing something. "I'll audition different people for the parts."

"Thanks. That will be a big help, Charlie."

Charlie became very busy, going to students' homes and auditioning them for different roles. He went to Sarah and Roger Bullard's house and chose them to be Mary and Joseph. Next, Charlie chose the shepherds, feeling quite proud of his progress. He then went to Jackie's house to see what she could do.

Jackie was *so* overdramatic in her audition, and she could only sing in a croak. Charlie was quite frightened.

"Ah...Jackie," he said, "is there anything else you can do? I'm afraid we've already got enough actors and singers."

"Oh, *yes,*" Jackie said. "I can do gorgeous makeup and hairdos. Just let me do it for all the actors and actresses before they perform."

"Great idea!" said Charlie thankfully. "I'm sure you're very good at that."

Charlie left Jackie's house and went to the Milliards' farm. The Milliards were kind people and were happy to lend their donkey and sheep for the pageant.

Now he just needed to find an angel. But he already knew where to look!

He hurried to Prissy's house. She was busy picking material to sew all the costumes with.

"Charlie," she said, "I'd appreciate it if you would ask all the actors and actresses to come to my house tomorrow. I need to get all their measurements for the costumes."

"Sure," said Charlie.

The cook gave him a sandwich, and as he ate it, he watched Prissy closely. She had blue eyes and golden hair. She was perfect for an angel! Claire was going to be the narrator, so that meant Prissy was the only choice for the role.

Prissy felt Charlie staring at her and looked up from her sewing. "What's the matter?" she asked. "Am I doing something wrong?"

"Oh, no. I was wondering if you would like to be the angel in the Christmas pageant. You certainly look the part."

"Oh, I know I do," Prissy said proudly. "Sure, I'll play the part. It would suit me the best."

"Oh, I don't know," Charlie said, getting up with a sly grin. "You better practice. You've got some pretty good competition with Claire around!"

Prissy was about to ask Charlie if that was true, but Charlie had gone off with a giggle. Oh well. She'd practice her angelic faces just in case!

Charlie felt pleased. He had someone to play each part, and he felt sure the pageant would be a hit. They were going to have their first rehearsal next week. He couldn't wait!

Next week came, and everyone was busy setting up the props for the rehearsal. Everyone admired the props Abel had made, especially the small-sized inn which his father had helped him build.

Prissy's costumes were amazing! Everyone admired them, especially the angel costume. Prissy had worked the hardest on the angel costume since she was going to wear it!

Pat had trained the barn animals remarkably well. They listened to his commands and knew where to during all the scenes.

The script was a big hit. Everyone loved it. Claire had done a fantastic job. She had written all the songs, and the church pianist had given them each a tune. The pianist was going to play the piano for the pageant, and she offered to help the actors and actresses learn the music. Claire shook with excitement. Her play was going to be performed. Just think of it!

Everyone was pleased with what they had done...except for one person. And that person was Charlie.

As Charlie looked at the costumes, the props, the script, and Pat training the animals, he couldn't help but think of how little he had done. He began to wonder...what was his talent? He had never bothered about it before, but now he did. Everyone seemed to have a talent but him!

He felt disappointed and very sad. As the rehearsal started, he watched the actors and actresses in their dazzling costumes with the beautiful props and scenery behind. He listened to Claire narrate her beautiful work and saw the animals listen to Pat's every command. Normally, Charlie would be the one running here and there, helping everybody; but he felt too moody to do that today.

He left the lawn, with its music and laughter, and went by himself inside the school where he would be far away...far from everyone's talent.

He quietly slid into his seat at the back of the classroom. Miss Jane was there, cleaning out the bookshelf.

"Charlie, what are you doing here?" she asked, walking over to him. "Surely you don't miss school that much! Why are you not with the others, practicing the pageant?"

Charlie looked up, startled. He hadn't realized that Miss Jane was there.

He sighed. "I'm not doing anything for the play," he said. "I just go with the flow!"

Miss Jane raised her eyebrows, surprised at Charlie's irritated tone. Charlie was usually so good-natured. Whatever was the matter?

"Charlie," she said, "is something bothering you? Would you like to talk to me about it?"

Charlie sighed again. "It's just that...it's just that everyone but me is so involved in the play. They all have great talents to use, talents that I don't have. Claire wrote the entire script and the songs by herself. Prissy made beautiful costumes. Abel made all the props and the scenery, and Pat trained all the animals. I did nothing compared to what they did! I'm just a lazy boy who likes to eat and is good at nothing. It's just not fair."

Miss Jane was surprised. "But Charlie," she said, "that's not true. You have so many talents that are very, very special!"

"Like what?" asked Charlie, very curious to know what his hidden talent might be.

"Well, you're very good-natured, and you're not in the least proud. You are always willing to help and are quite a good helper when you want to be. You're great at finding out others' talents and encouraging them, too. Who would have thought that shy little Sharon had such a beautiful voice until you discovered it!"

"But that's not the same," Charlie said. "It's nothing special."

"Oh yes, it is. Every gift comes from God, which makes every gift special. God doesn't compare the talents of one person with those of another. He just wants us to serve Him and others with them wholeheartedly. A talent can be very special, but if we don't glorify God with it, it's useless. And from what I've seen, Charlie, I'd say that you use your talents to serve God and others wholeheartedly."

Charlie thought for a while and then smiled. "You're right, Miss Jane," he said. "I've been silly to be jealous of others' talents. I'll use mine to glorify God and be thankful for the talents he's given me."

"That's right, Charlie," Miss Jane smiled. "Now...how are you going to glorify God with your talents?"

Charlie got up. "By helping all I can with the rehearsal that's taking place outside!" he said with a grin.

Chapter Eleven: Our Heavenly Father

"For you formed my inward parts; You knitted me together in my mother's womb. I praise you, for I am fearfully and wonderfully made. Wonderful are your works; my soul knows it very well."
Psalm 139:13-14

"Father, you have to meet my very special friend, Claire! And Claire, this is my father...the best father I could ever ask for!"

Claire, who had just been about to enter the schoolhouse for class that morning, turned and looked at the tall, handsome, sophisticated looking man who had accompanied Prissy to the schoolhouse. His blue eyes twinkled, and Claire liked his friendly smile.

"Hello, Claire," Mr. Robinson said, politely shaking Claire's hand. "It's very nice to meet you. I'm glad to see my daughter has made such a fine friend!"

"Oh, Mr. Robinson, *I'm* the one who's glad to have such a nice friend like Prissy," Claire said sincerely. "She sure is pretty amazing."

"I don't doubt it," Mr. Robinson said, proudly smiling down at his daughter and pulling her close.

"Father came back from his business trip in Europe just yesterday," Prissy told Claire. "I'm *so* happy! You'll be home for Christmas, Father!"

"I could never imagine spending it away from you, my love," Mr. Robinson said. "I'm glad to be home, too. My trip was long, *much* too long. But you know, dear, I always kept a picture of you with me, and I was constantly thinking about you. And now, we have all the time in the world to spend with each other!"

Prissy laughed with delight and gave her father a hug. Claire watched them, a longing look in her eyes and a wistful smile on her lips. What she would do to have *her* father home for Christmas.

****

"A penny for your thoughts," Miss Jane said that afternoon after school as she set a plate of freshly baked cookies before Claire, who was sitting at the kitchen table. The girl was resting her cheek against her hand and seemed lost in her own world.

Claire smiled. "Thanks, Miss Jane," she said, taking a cookie. She nibbled on it with hardly any enthusiasm, Miss Jane noted. And Claire *never* ate her chocolate chip cookies in such a manner!

"What's wrong, Claire?" the schoolteacher asked the girl kindly.

Claire let out a big sigh. "Miss Jane, every day I hope my father will come for me," she said. "And whenever Christmas rolls around, I wish that even more. I know I'm being silly, because now, I have you, Aunt Ellen, and so many friends who love me. But I can't help missing my father...even though I've never even met him."

Claire's voice shook slightly. "I've created such wonderful stories about him...how he's doing all sorts of grand things. But I...I think the truth is...if my father is alive, he...he doesn't really care about me. Otherwise, he'd be searching for me. He'd have found me by now. I've been on my own for nearly twelve years."

Miss Jane took a seat next to Claire, gently taking her hand in hers. Claire looked up at her with dark, soulful eyes.

"Why can't I have a father?" she asked in a choked voice. "A *real* father?"

Miss Jane was silent for several minutes. "Claire," she said finally, "what's everything you wish for in a father?"

"He'd truly love me, truly care about me," Claire answered. "He'd know everything there is to know about me...all my likes and dislikes. He'd always be there for me when I need someone to talk to. He'd never be too busy for me, ever. He'd do anything to protect me. And...and...maybe, he'd even have a picture of me that he'd always keep with him. He'd just love me a lot, you see, and would always keep me close to his heart."

Miss Jane smiled. "Claire," she said gently, "you *do* have that kind of father."

Claire looked up at Miss Jane. "My Heavenly Father?"

Miss Jane nodded. "You know, Claire, He knows everything there is to know about you...all your likes and dislikes. The Bible says that He knew you even before you were in the womb, and He tenderly knit you together. He takes such great joy in you that He even rejoices over you with singing."

"Really?" Claire said, deeply touched. She had never thought of herself as something anyone would sing about.

"Really," Miss Jane said. "He's never too busy for you, Claire, because He cares about you, and He treasures you. You are the apple of His eye, and there's never a time you can't talk to Him about something. He *would* do anything to protect you...He even gave up His life on the cross to save you from eternal death. And dear, He has more than just a picture of you which He always keeps with Him; the Bible says He has engraved you on the palms of His hands. You are *always* close to His heart."

Claire's eyes filled with tears. "You're right, Miss Jane," she said. "I have a father who's more than anything I could ever imagine. I haven't really been on my own all these years. He promises never to leave me, and He's here with me right now. He's always been there for me, and He always will be. I am His."

The schoolteacher and girl embraced. Claire's heart was filled with the warmth of a happiness words could not describe—a happiness that came from knowing she was forever in the arms of her Heavenly Daddy, who would never let her go.

Chapter Twelve: A Grand Christmas Celebration

" For to us a child is born, to us a son is given; and the government shall be upon his shoulder, and his name shall be called Wonderful, Counselor, Mighty God, Everlasting Father, Prince of Peace." Isaiah 9:6

The days flew by, and the Christmas Eve dinner was fast approaching. It was now the day before it, and the children were beginning their very last rehearsal for the pageant.

"Where in the world are Abel and Pat?" Claire said for the twentieth time. "Abel needs to see if his costume fits him, and Pat has to get the animals ready."

"Claire! Oh, Claire, the animals are going wild backstage. I'm trying to calm them down. The sheep are trying to eat all the costumes!" Charlie was red and was panting hard.

"Dearie me!" Claire exclaimed, running to where the animals were gathered. "Oh, blow! You naughty sheep, you've torn the angel's costume! Oh, where is Pat? I told him clearly that the rehearsal was at ten o'clock! Ouch! Oh, you donkey, don't you dare butt me like that again!"

"Claire, the tear is big," Prissy cried, examining the costume. "I don't know if I can fix it in time."

"Claire, the tear is big," Prissy cried

"Prissy, you've got to do something," Claire said urgently. "You can't appear on stage with a big tear in the front!"

"I don't know, Claire. I'll try to get it fixed. I feel like smacking those sheep! It was hateful of them, especially as I worked so hard to sew it, too!"

Pat appeared just then with Abel, and they were greeted by a furious Claire.

"Where were you two? I told you specifically that the rehearsal was at ten. You've held us all up, and we've wasted precious time. Pat, the animals are going nuts!"

"Sorry, Claire," Pat said, running to calm the animals.

"Prissy, Claire!" said Sarah, running toward them. "I've just got news that Sharon has got a sore throat from being outside in the cold too long. She was to sing a solo, wasn't she?"

Claire felt as if she had been shot. "It can't be true!" she said, almost crying. "Sharon has a major part in the pageant. She's got to come. Whatever are we to do?"

Sarah shrugged her shoulders. "We should probably just cancel the pageant," she said. "Everything's going wrong."

"No. We won't cancel anything. We'll go on with it, even if it's absolutely terrible."

Sarah went away, shaking her head. Claire looked at Prissy in despair. Prissy smiled sympathetically.

"Don't get too worked up," she said. "I'll get Mother to help me fix the costume. If Sharon isn't well by tomorrow night, we can just have the pianist play pretty carols—you know, the ones she played in church a few days ago. Everything will be all right, Claire."

Prissy's calmness and confidence seemed to soothe Claire. But her peace didn't last long.

"Claire, don't be upset," said Charlie, running to her, looking very distraught. "Something very horrible has happened."

"What?" Claire asked, alarmed.

"I think you better sit down."

"Oh dear, it's really that bad is it?" Claire said, sitting down.

"Yes. Well, Anna-Lee and Jacob had a pretty bad argument just now, and Anna-Lee declared she'd never speak to him again. She insists that she won't even be able to speak to him on stage when they're playing Mary and Joseph."

"What?!"

"Now, Claire, don't get all mad. You know Anna-Lee's temper always dies down pretty soon."

"Charlie, how can you be so calm? The entire pageant depends on them! They've *got* to say their lines. There isn't enough time for them to while away playing dumb charades!"

Claire jumped up, but Charlie pushed her down. He knew Claire's temper.

"Now, Claire, don't get worked up. We've already got too many fiery tempers to deal with."

Abel came running up. "Hello, hello," he said, looking at Claire's angry face. "Claire, you look about ready to explode!"

Claire jumped up again but was promptly pushed back down by Charlie.

Prissy was quite worried. "Abel, Anna-Lee and Joseph are refusing to say their lines because they're mad at each other."

"What?"

"Yes, it's true. What are we going to do?"

"Everything's going wrong!" Claire cried, tears welling up in her eyes.

"Claire, don't," Abel said. "Poor thing, you're quite stressed out. Charlie and I will pacify Anna-Lee and Jacob, you'll see."

They left, and Prissy stayed with Claire. She wasn't much help, unfortunately, for she was often subject to hysterics and was just about to lose control of herself when Abel and Charlie came running toward them. They both jumped up when they saw the boys.

"You won't believe it," Abel said, laughing. "Anna-Lee was mad at Jacob because he said that in her Mary costume, she made even the donkey she rode on look good. Anna-Lee thought he was saying she looked so hideous, even the donkey looked better than her; but he only meant that she looked so good, the ugly donkey didn't look half as bad with her on him. It was just a misunderstanding they had. They're friends, now."

"Thank goodness!" said Claire, wiping her brow. "Then let's begin the rehearsal. Quick, Abel, get changed!"

The rehearsal was dreadful. The donkey threw Mary off of him and stepped on Joseph's toes. The shepherds completely forgot their lines. The sheep ran around butting each other, and it took Pat a long time to control them. Charlie ran into Abel, and they both fell with a thud. And Jackie, the makeup and hair designer, spilled her face powder all over Prissy's hair.

"Oh!" Claire groaned afterward, "we'll never be ready for tomorrow!"

No one dared to disagree with her. Everyone was feeling pretty low. Would tomorrow's performance be a complete disaster?

****

The next day, Miss Jane worked hard for hours, cooking, and making the house look Christmassy.

Claire had gone over to meet Prissy's mother, and was absolutely enchanted with the charming, pretty woman. Mrs. Robinson was quite kind about helping repair the angel costume, reassuring the girls that she could have it repaired in time.

Charlie's mother was helping Miss Jane prepare the food, and Miss Jane was quite grateful for her. Mrs. Thompson was an excellent cook and was famous in town for her abilities as a chef.

Charlie himself was visiting Sharon. Generous and thoughtful, he had remembered sick little Sharon and was at her house, offering her his mother's sore throat remedy—delicious, hot chicken soup. The boy hoped it would work its magic and heal Sharon of her sore throat.

Pat was busy giving the animals last-minute instructions, and Abel was making sure that all of his special props were not broken.

Then it was time. The Christmas Eve dinner was ready, and many people filled Miss Jane's house. The guests chatted and laughed together, enjoying one another's company.

Miss Jane's house was right next to the school lawn where the pageant was going to be performed. Many plays were performed on the school lawn because of the big stage that stood at the center of it. Miss Jane's guests, all bundled up in jackets and scarves, went outside and soon filled up the rows of chairs arranged in front of the stage.

Meanwhile, chaos reigned behind the curtains. Everyone ran here and there, changing into costumes and rehearsing their lines. Sharon was there, her eyes sparkling with excitement. Her voice had come back, thanks to Charlie's mother's marvelous healing concoction. It was the first time she would be singing in front of an audience, and she was quite nervous.

Pat was calming the animals, as they were getting restless, sensing the excitement. He patted them, hugged them, cried over them, and told them how proud he was of them and how this was the biggest moment of their lives. Basically, he "behaved as if they were his children," Abel said later.

Abel himself was all dressed up as an innkeeper. He wore a white-haired wig and a white beard which made him quite unrecognizable.

Prissy looked beautiful, and she knew it. Her mother had fixed the costume gorgeously so that the tear could not even be seen. The silver sequins sparkled in the light and reflected off of her pretty, dark blue eyes. Her golden hair was curled and fixed most elegantly, thanks to Jackie.

Indeed, Jackie had quite a gift, as the others discovered that night. She knew the exact hairstyles and makeup that would suit each person and make them look like how their character was supposed to look.

Claire was panic stricken, although she didn't show it. She went around encouraging the others and made life easier for the nervous actors and actresses. She was dressed in a pretty red Christmas dress. She had insisted on tying her hair back in braids, but Jackie had objected, saying it looked too ordinary. Claire had tried arguing with her, telling her that she *was* ordinary and didn't want to be dolled up like Prissy, but Jackie wouldn't have it. So, Claire gave in and allowed herself to be "dolled up," and she looked quite nice.

Charlie was helping all he could, using his gift to the best of his ability. Claire was very grateful for him that night, for he seemed to know that she *was* nervous, and he eased her anxiety by doing anything and everything that the cast needed.

Soon it was time for the show to begin. Claire went out with the script in her hands, shaking with nervousness. But as time went on, she got bolder and bolder, reading the narration so beautifully and with such feeling and emotion that everyone applauded when she had finished.

Next came in Prissy, the beautiful angel, reciting Luke chapter two and telling Mary that she would give birth to Jesus. Everyone admired the costume as much as her performance.

When Mary and Joseph entered, with Mary riding on the donkey, the audience gasped. A real donkey in the play—how incredible! Pat, watching nervously behind the curtains, let out a breath of relief when the donkey was done doing his part. "Good!" he thought. "All is going perfectly!"

Then came the innkeeper and his wife, played by Abel and Charlie, who was dressed up like a girl. They allowed Mary and Joseph to have the barn for the night.

The shepherds came in next and did their comedy act, which sent everyone laughing. The sheep were very well behaved and made their way off stage without incident. Prissy and two other angels then sang "Gloria," harmonizing beautifully with one another.

Then, they were all at the manger, where everyone sang "Away in a Manger." Claire came out and read Isaiah 9:6, and then it was over. It was really over.

The audience stood to their feet, clapping loudly as all the actors and actresses came and took a bow. Abel, Pat, Charlie, Prissy and Claire all smiled at each other. The pageant had been a great success.

They all went behind the curtains, changed out of their costumes, and went back into the house for a lovely Christmas Eve dinner. Three big turkeys were served, and a variety of other meat. There was cold potato salad, lemonade, warm bread with butter, and all kinds of other foods, with cookies and chocolate fudge cake for dessert. Delicious!

But the best part of the evening was when they all went into town to give blankets, Bibles, and food to the homeless people there and share the gospel with them.

"You know something, Prissy?" Claire said as they watched a young boy cry with happiness over his gifts.

"What's that, Claire?'

"I think this is the best Christmas Eve I've ever had."

"Yeah, me too," Prissy replied with a joyous smile and bright eyes.

And indeed, it was.

Chapter Thirteen: God's Eternal Love

"Do not love the world or the things in the world. If anyone loves the world, the love of the Father is not in him. For all that is in the world—the desires of the flesh and the desires of the eyes and pride of life—is not from the Father but is from the world. And the world is passing away along with its desires, but whoever does the will of God abides forever." 1 John 2:15-17

The two weeks of Christmas vacation passed by quickly. It was time to go back to school. The students came back yawning tiredly, still dreaming of sugarplums and candy canes. No one was thrilled to return. That was always the hardest part about vacations.

Miss Jane didn't want to come back either. She was in a terrible mood. She had gone to bed with the Christmas spirit and was forced to wake up in the morning with the regular school-day attitude. She could never get used to such a transition.

"But I mustn't be grumpy," she thought. "The children will already be feeling pretty low. I won't make them work too hard today. We'll have a fun Math competition and a Geography bee."

So, Miss Jane got ready, packed her lunch, and went to school, determined that the first day back was going to be a good day.

Her students were waiting for her when she arrived. She quickly went to her desk and took attendance. She looked at her class, noting the usual effects of a long vacation.

Charlie was sleeping on his desk, a candy cane hanging out of his mouth. Prissy had unbelievably forgotten to comb her hair and was yawning nonstop. Claire and Abel were in wild tempers about something and were arguing their heads off. And Pat was busy playing with a collar his parents had given him for his pet frog, George.

Miss Jane rapped on her desk, but nobody paid attention.

"Class," Miss Jane called out, hoping *someone* would hear her. "Class, it's time for school to begin...class!"

Miss Jane sighed. "Well, guess I've got to do what I've got to do," the schoolteacher thought to herself. She put her fingers in her mouth and let out a loud, high-pitched whistle, causing everyone to jump in surprise.

"Ah...hello, class," Miss Jane said. "Now, since I have your attention, could you please all go to your seats so we can begin our school day?"

There was a loud scramble for seats, and Miss Jane waited until the shuffling of feet had stopped before continuing.

"I hope that everyone had a lovely break, and I welcome you all back to school. I understand that coming back to work after a long vacation can be tough, but your final exams are coming up, and I know you all want to do well. I've no doubt that you will, but we've really got no time to slack, as I'm sure you'll all agree."

The class looked at their schoolteacher in silence. Yes, they all badly wanted to do well on their final exams, but it was so hard to think about tests at the moment.

"Blah," Pat said at recess as he and his friends sat under the big oak tree in the schoolyard, eating their lunch. "That's how I feel every year after Christmas. Blah."

"It's the post-Christmas blues," Abel said. "After the holidays, there's nothing to look forward to anymore. Everyone's done being nice and cheery and giving out gifts. We all go back to our grumpy selves."

"It shouldn't be that way," Claire said determinedly. "I think we should always show others God's love, even if it's not Christmas-time. Christ came to earth and was born in a manger, but the story doesn't end there! He saved us, and His love was born in our hearts. We've got to live out His love every day!"

"Oooh, that's good," Charlie, who had been enjoying the sandwich his mother made him, said, his mouth full. "However do you come up with such clever-sounding things?"

"Thanks, Charlie," Claire said with a grin, giving her friend a playful punch on the arm.

"You're right, Claire," Abel said. "We *should* continue showing God's love...and I've got the best idea!"

"What?" everyone asked curiously.

"Well, you know how we met a lot of homeless kids in town on Christmas Eve when we went around handing out Bibles, blankets, and food?" Abel asked. Everyone nodded. "Well, I think we should all collect more things for them...toys and anything they might like. We could ask Miss Jane if we could set up a donation box at the back of the classroom, maybe, and everyone could give a little something...you know, things they no longer use that are still in good condition, or even brand new things."

"What a fabulous idea!" Claire cried.

"Marvelous," Pat agreed.

"I really have such clever friends," Charlie said.

"Er...yes, that's a good idea," Prissy said, sounding a little worried. But everyone else was too excited to notice.

"Let's go ask Miss Jane if she'll let us set up a donation box," Claire said, jumping to her feet as everyone followed suit. "C'mon!"

****

Miss Jane thought the children's idea was very kind and thoughtful, and a donation box was set at the back of the classroom. Donations flooded in, including Pat's red toy car, Abel's best shoes, a box of chocolates form Charlie, and Claire's picture-book she had loved as a little girl.

Prissy, however, could not seem to find anything she wanted to give! The poor girl really *did* want to give something special to the kids they were raising donations for...only, she loved her possessions so much, she didn't think she could part with anything.

"Let's see now," Prissy said to herself one Saturday morning, looking at the rows of pink dresses in her closet. "I have so many dresses, I could probably give away one. I'll give away this one, maybe...but oh, I look *ever* so beautiful in it! And I can't give the silk dress away, it's so expensive. Maybe the lace one will do...but no, it really suits my figure the best. Oh dear. why must everything be so difficult?"

Prissy spent several hours wrestling with herself, trying to find something she wouldn't mind parting with. But there were no pairs of shoes, no hair-ribbons, and certainly no jewelry she could bid farewell to.

"I feel awful about it, Miss Jane," Prissy told the schoolteacher later that afternoon during a visit to her house. "Everyone else has something to give the kids, but I can't seem to find anything."

Miss Jane listened as she began to set the table for tea. Prissy helped her, setting a dish of freshly baked butter buns on the table.

"It's just that everything I own is so costly," Prissy said. "I...I don't mean to sound snobbish, Miss Jane, but...I really can't part with things that hold such great value, can I?"

Miss Jane looked at the pretty girl, who started back at her with large blue eyes. "Prissy," the schoolteacher said kindly, "nothing has the power to be worth more than the value you place on it. It doesn't matter whether or not your possessions are costly and expensive...*you're* the one who truly assigns any value to them."

"Do you think I'm placing too much value on my things?" Prissy asked.

Miss Jane smiled. "All I know is that what we value should align with what our Heavenly Father values; that's truly what matters, in the end. And more than anything, God values every person, because we are all created in His image. There's nothing more important to Him than a person's soul. What a wonderful thing it is to value other people in the same way...so much so, that the value we place on our possessions pales in comparison."

Prissy looked down, the words Miss Jane had spoken resonating in her heart. The schoolteacher gently lifted the girl's chin and looked into her eyes.

"Prissy, God's love *is* costly. Having His love in us requires us not to place a high value on the things of this world. But my dear, when our eyes are on Christ—the one who values us so much, He gave His all to save us—we'll find that God deserves all of us...our whole heart. Nothing else in this world deserves *any* part of our heart. We do everything because we love Him who first loved us. We are willing to give up the things of this world that are fading away because our Heavenly Father has given us what we could never lose—Jesus."

Prissy smiled back at the schoolteacher. "Thanks, Miss Jane," she said gratefully. "I think you've really helped me get my priorities straight!"

And so, it was with a happier, generous spirit that Prissy donated one of her favorite dolls. She would always like the pretty things she had, but they no longer controlled a part of her heart. Her love belonged to Jesus and the precious people He had created. And in valuing her Savior, it was then that Prissy found her own true value—value in the One who gave up everything so she could be a child of the Most High King.

Chapter Fourteen: Burt the Bully

"But the Lord said to Samuel, "Do not look on his appearance or on the height of his stature, because I have rejected him. For the Lord sees not as man sees: man looks on the outward appearance, but the Lord looks on the heart." 1 Samuel 16:7

News spreads quickly in a small town, and before long, everyone knew that Parson Andrews and his wife were moving. This was quite sad, of course, as everyone was rather fond of the family. But a parson was needed in another church a few towns away, and Parson Andrews had accepted the offer.

"This Sunday will be the last one my wife and I will be spending with you," he had announced from the pulpit a couple of Sundays ago. "As most of you already know, Parson David Hanson will be taking my place. Please welcome him into the church as a brother and a leader."

Parson David, or Parson Davy as everyone called him, was in his late twenties. He was quite friendly and jolly, and everyone accepted him into the community at once.

"I quite like Parson Davy," Pat declared one day when they were all having tea at Miss Jane's house. "He's exactly my idea of what I think a parson should be. You know, he gave me a dollar yesterday, a whole dollar, just for reciting a bible verse by memory!"

"And did you know he likes Shakespeare too?" asked Claire, whose idea of a parson was a person who diligently studied the Bible for hours and had no time or interest in reading poetic books. "We had quite a nice conversation yesterday about him. Parson Davy thinks he was a great writer."

"Do you like him, Miss Jane?" Abel asked.

"Shakespeare or Parson Davy?"

"Parson Davy, of course!" Abel said with a grin.

"Yes, I do," Miss Jane said, smiling in return at her student and stopping to fill everyone's cup with tea. "He preached a wonderful sermon last Sunday, and I've no doubt he's a fine man."

The students smiled at each other. Good! It was a wonderful sign if Miss Jane liked him. Miss Jane always seemed to know the good and trustable people, and whoever she liked, they did too!

They were just finishing their tea when they heard a knock at the door. "I'll get it," Prissy said, jumping out of her chair. She ran to the door and opened it.

"Oh, Parson Davy," she said. "Hello!"

"Hello, Prissy! Is Miss Jane here?"

"Yes. She's in the kitchen."

Miss Jane, hearing her name mentioned, hurried to the door. "Oh, Parson Davy," she said with her pleasant smile. "Is there anything I can do for you?"

Parson Davy returned the smile. "Good day, Miss Jane," he said. "I hear you're the teacher of the school here. I was wondering if you'd let me see the school?"

"Oh, certainly," said Miss Jane, wiping her hands on her apron. "Follow me. The school's right next door."

Miss Jane walked to the school, and Parson Davy followed her. She put her key into the lock and pushed open the school door.

"Well, here you are," said Miss Jane, her eyes shining with pride. "This is our school."

Parson Davy looked with interest at the desks and chairs that were neatly arranged in rows, where students would sit under Miss Jane's watchful eye.

"Do many students attend school here?" he asked.

"Well yes, quite a few. Five of the students are at the house if you would like to speak with them."

"Yes, I would," Parson Davy said. "I've seen them all in church before. They seem like nice kids."

Parson Davy looked around the school once more. "This is quite a nice school you've got, Miss Jane," he said. "I've heard a lot about it and you."

Miss Jane laughed. "Good things, I hope?" she asked.

"Oh yes. Many say you're a wonderful teacher and that they love the way you touch each child's life."

Miss Jane blushed. "Oh, that's really sweet. I just try my best to point the kids to Jesus. He's really the One who makes a difference in all of us."

"And that is why I want to know if you'd allow one more student to attend this school. You've got the thing that really counts."

Miss Jane raised her eyebrows in interest. "One more student?" she said. "Who?"

Parson Davy grinned. "Well, my nephew, Burt Eddleton, moved in with me last Monday. His parents are in a bit of financial trouble, having lost their savings when they made some poor investments. They haven't been able to provide Burt with the education they would like him to have. I offered to take Burt in until they got back on their feet. Burt's never been to a school like this one, but you'll let him come to yours, won't you?"

"Of course," Miss Jane said. "I will be happy to have him. I'm sure he'll settle in after a few weeks."

"I hope so," Parson Davy said, looking a bit nervous. "Burt's got his good points, but he's rather difficult and quite rambunctious at the moment. I think he might cause some disturbances in class, and...well...he looks like he can be a bit of a bully."

"Oh, don't worry!" Miss Jane said, laughing. "I know how to deal with that kind of behavior. And I'm sure the children would understand too, for they're all kind souls, especially the five children at my house. Burt will be quite all right, I'm sure."

"Well, all right," said Parson Davy, looking reassured. "Burt will start school on Monday."

****

"Good morning, class," Miss Jane said on Monday morning. "We have a new addition to our class, as many of you have noticed. This is Burt Eddleton. We're very excited to have you, Burt. Aren't we class?"

"Yes, Miss Jane," the class said, looking at the newcomer with interest. He was tall with broad shoulders. He had blonde hair and fierce brown eyes. He stared back at them defiantly. Claire giggled as she looked at him and then at Abel, who was also looking rather grim. Abel very much thought the rebellious-looking boy needed to be sat on. There would be a jolly good fight if they didn't watch out!

"Well, I'm not glad to be here!" Burt said. "I don't need school. I'll jolly well show you how much I already know. I bet I'm way smarter than the lot of you."

"Now just you watch what you say!" said Abel, jumping to his feet and shaking a fist. "You just be careful, or I'll..."

"Abel!" said Miss Jane sharply. "Abel, sit down. That's not the way to behave, and you know that. Please apologize to Burt."

"But Miss Jane, I..."

"Abel!"

"I'm sorry!" Abel said, not in the least bit remorseful, sitting down sulkily.

"As for you, Burt," Miss Jane said. "You may know a lot, but everyone is treated equally at this school, and you should respect everyone, whether you know more than them or not. Now, is there anywhere you would particularly like to sit?"

"I don't want to sit here, stand here, or be here. I want to..."

"All right, Burt, you can tell me what you want to do *after* class."

Prissy shook her head and curled a golden lock around her finger. She knew that this was a school where everyone was treated equally...but really! Couldn't this boy at least put on some decent clothes before he came to school? He said he knew a lot, but to her, it certainly didn't look like he knew how to dress!

"I know the perfect spot for you," Miss Jane said, eyeing Prissy closely. "I'll put you next to Prissy. You'll see to it that Burt's made comfortable, won't you Prissy?"

Prissy looked up, horrified. What?! Have this new, rebellious bully sit next to her? Never!

"But Miss Jane, I...well, you see..."

"Yes, Prissy?"

"Well..."

"Well, you think that would be a splendid idea? I couldn't agree with you more!"

Prissy bit her lip and went pale. She couldn't very well say that she hated the idea of sitting next to Burt, could she? Oh, dear! Why did Miss Jane have to choose her?

Claire looked at her and grinned, but quickly stopped when she saw Miss Jane looking at her. She didn't want to sit next to Burt any more than Prissy did!

Burt reluctantly went and sat next to Prissy, taking with him his textbooks and school supplies.

Prissy moved as far away from him as possible. Burt grinned. "You're one of those mighty rich kids, aren't you?" he whispered in her ear. "Make way for the queen! I'm so humbled to sit next to you, Your Highness."

"Oh! How dare you!" Prissy exclaimed. "You're the rudest boy I've ever met. Talk to me after you've learned the twelve times table!"

Burt grinned and shrugged his shoulders. Who cared what this rich little donkey said? Definitely not him!

School was very exciting that day. Prissy couldn't stop grumbling under her breath. Claire got called out for giggling. Abel kept clenching his fist. Charlie, as usual, was in his own world, dreaming of candies. Pat got reprimanded for whispering to his neighbor about the "new kid." But Burt...he was the worst of the lot.

He kept disrupting Miss Jane's class. He tied Prissy's hair to the back of her chair while she was doing her Math sums so that Prissy found, to her astonishment, that she couldn't stand to answer the Math sums on the board. He scribbled over Claire's beloved book, and Claire exploded like a pressure cooker. He stole Charlie's candies and ate every single one of them. He grabbed George from Pat and held him tightly in his hand so that the poor frog couldn't escape. This outraged Pat, who loved his beloved pets, and when he told Miss Jane what Burt had done and got George back, Burt nicknamed him "Tell-tale" and called him that for the entire day. At recess, Burt pushed Abel from a tree, which angered the boy greatly. "I'll get you back for that, Burt Eddleton!" Abel had cried. And he meant what he said.

****

The next day was not a very good one for Burt, as Claire, Abel, Prissy, Pat and Charlie had determined to get back at him for all the nasty things he had done.

First, Charlie had stuck gum on Burt's chair so that when Burt got up to do the sums on the board, the class saw a hilarious sight. Everyone burst out laughing. Burt turned very red once he realized what the class was laughing at.

Miss Jane was very angry. "Who did this?" she demanded.

No one said anything. "If the culprit doesn't own up, the whole class will have to stay in for recess."

Charlie looked at the others in dismay, and they looked back at him, sympathy on their faces. He slowly stood up. "I did it, Miss Jane," he said.

"See me after class," Miss Jane said grimly. "And see to it that you apologize to Burt and clean up the rest of the gum from his chair."

"Yes, ma'am," said Charlie, turning pinker than any gum in the world.

When Burt returned to his seat, he found an envelope in his desk addressed to "Burt Eddleton." He opened it and read the poem that had been stuck inside it. Unbeknownst to him, it had been written by Claire.

Burt the Bully

We lived our days quite happily,
In the class of Miss Jane,
But then came Burt the bully,
And he caused us much deep pain.

He ate all Charlie's candy,
And him he never repaid,
And poor Charlie's pockets were empty,
Because of how badly Burt behaved.

He tied Prissy's hair to her chair,
And Prissy was very upset,
But Burt the bully didn't care,
And he did something ruder yet.

Pat's beloved pet friend he took,
And Pat began to wail,
He told Miss Jane the deed of the crook,
And Burt called him "Tell-Tale."

He pushed Abel from a tree,
During recess,
And he laughed so happily,
Never after did he confess.

So were the sins of Mr. Eddleton,
The lives of many he hurt,
Being with him was not very fun,
And everyone grew tired of Burt.

Then the day finally came,
When Miss Jane had good news to tell,
And nothing was the same,
After Burt, she did expel.

Never again we'd hear his voice,

Never again Burt we'd see,
And though we all did rejoice,
The happiest of all was
ME.

Burt read the poem twice and gave an angry grunt. He could not for the life of him think of who wrote it, for it had not been signed. He got up and went to Miss Jane's desk to show the letter to her.

Miss Jane took the letter and read it, a frown coming over her face. She knew who the culprit was! No one could have made the words rhyme so cleverly yet gotten her point through in great depth, except for...Claire! Miss Jane read the poem again and tried to keep herself from smiling. Yes, she knew the poem was very mean and had an ill intention behind it, but she could not help but admire the intelligent play of words and think it was just a little funny. "Thank you, Burt," she said quickly. "I'm sorry this has happened to you. If you don't mind, I'd like to keep this. I think I know who the culprit is, and I'd like to have a few words with her."

Miss Jane looked at Claire and knew that she was listening, although she was pretending to work very hard on her Math problems. The little monkey!

Burt was having quite a terrible day, but the worst was yet to come. Now it was Pat's turn to do *his* evil work.

The class was learning about snakes in Science class. Pat was very interested. Pat loved snakes, as he did all animals, and even had his own pet snake named Sally.

"Now, listen," Pat whispered to Abel, who was his desk partner. "I've got Sally with me. I'll slip her into Burt's Science textbook during recess, and when Burt opens it later, he'll have a wonderful surprise!"

Abel grinned. So, Pat, true to his word, lay Sally all coiled up in the middle of Burt's book, closing it carefully so Sally wouldn't get squished.

Sadly for Pat, things didn't work out as he had planned, and he soon landed in a lot of trouble. After the break, the class seated themselves at their desks once again. They were all looking forward to the Science lesson Miss Jane was to teach, for Science was a subject well-liked by all the students.

"Now, class," Miss Jane said, resuming her lesson, "please open your Science textbooks to page seventy-one."

Prissy rummaged inside her desk, finding to her dismay that her Science textbook was missing. "Excuse me, Miss Jane," she said, raising her hand. "I can't seem to find my textbook."

"Very well," Miss Jane said, not at all pleased, for she was an organized person and didn't like anything to be misplaced. "You may share Burt's textbook, as he is your desk partner."

Burt let out an exclamation. "I've got two books in my desk, Miss Jane," he said. "One must be Prissy's. Here you are, Prissy!"

Prissy retrieved the book gratefully and opened it. Sally, whose good temper was a little ruffled at having been pushed into the book, slithered out onto Prissy's desk, giving her a disapproving glare.

Now, Prissy didn't like snakes the way Pat did, thinking them grotesque. Seeing the snake, Prissy let out a piercing shriek and pushed her chair as far away as possible from her desk. Miss Jane jumped, dropping the chalk she had been using to write on the board, and turned around instantaneously.

"Prissy!" she said. "Why would you..."

"Oh, Miss Jane!" Prissy cried. "A snake slithered out from my textbook, and now it's on my desk!"

"Good gracious!" Miss Jane exclaimed, walking quickly toward Prissy's desk. "However did a snake get into your textbook?"

"I bet that wicked boy did it!" Prissy cried, pointing an accusing finger at Burt. "It's something he would do. He could have easily taken my textbook and put the snake in since he sits right next to me!"

"I didn't do it," Burt said, looking with amazement at the snake. "I think it's a jolly good idea, but I tell you, I didn't do it! I can't think how it got put in Prissy's textbook."

Pat stood up, very red in the face. As much as he wanted to get Burt into trouble, he couldn't let him take the blame for something he hadn't done. "I did it, Miss Jane," he said bravely.

"I wanted to give Burt a surprise, so I slipped it into a textbook in his desk, which happened to belong to Prissy. I'm sorry Prissy. I didn't mean for Sally to give *you* a shock!"

"Well, Pat!" Miss Jane exclaimed, not at all pleased. "That was a very mean thing to do! Please come and take this snake away, and let me never see it in my class again. And Pat, Prissy isn't the only one you should be apologizing to!"

"I'm sorry, Burt," Pat mumbled, quickly removing Sally and stuffing her into his bag.

Miss Jane continued teaching, and there were no more disturbances for the rest of the school day. Burt made out as if he didn't care in the least about how the others were treating him. He held his head up high and never once looked at the others. But Miss Jane was not deceived. She saw how his hand trembled when he wrote and perceived that his voice sounded less confident than usual. "I'll have a talk with Abel, Pat, Charlie, Prissy and Claire today," she thought to herself. "Burt's been punished enough. It's time he was given a chance!"

The day finally came to an end, and the class flooded gratefully out of the door, except for the five children who were told to stay behind.

Miss Jane sat at her desk, writing. The five children sat with nervous anticipation in their seats. Why, oh, why did Miss Jane leave them hanging in suspense for so long like this? Why didn't she scold them and get it all over with?

Miss Jane finally put her pen down and looked at them with her gentle brown eyes.

"If you think I'm going to scold and lecture you, you're wrong," Miss Jane began in a calm voice. "I'm not. Knowing you, you probably already feel terrible after what happened. What I just want to know is why you did all those awful things to Burt."

The children said nothing, not even Claire, who could usually always come up with a quick-witted answer.

Miss Jane drew out a piece of paper from her desk and showed it to the children. Claire gulped.

"Claire," Miss Jane began, "I reckon you know who wrote this?"

"Yes, Miss Jane," Claire mumbled. "I did."

Miss Jane sighed. "Claire, there are many things I admire about you. Your kindness, fairness, and talents are something that few people have. But Claire, it seems to me that you are not using your talents for God's glory. Do you think God gave you the talent of writing to write mean things about others? You are misusing your gifts, don't you see?"

Claire nodded her head miserably. "I'm sorry, Miss Jane," she said. "Sorry for writing those awful things about Burt. I won't ever do so again."

"And you," Miss Jane said, turning to Charlie. "Why would you stick gum on Burt's chair? You know gum is not even allowed in school."

Charlie looked down. "I know," he said solemnly.

"And Pat, surely you knew that sticking a snake in a textbook to give Burt a shock was not at all a wise thing to do. I suppose you knew what Pat was about to do, didn't you, Abel? Why didn't you stop him? Because you wanted to have some fun and see Burt get punished?

"Pat, Charlie, don't you remember that at the beginning of the year we had that talk about always doing what Jesus would do since we are His followers?"

Pat and Charlie nodded slowly.

"Well, my boys, you know that we must show God's love to everyone, and that includes Burt. And Prissy, why do you look down on Burt just because he is not as well off as you are? I think you can do better than that, don't you?"

Prissy nodded miserably. She *had* looked down on Burt and been awfully haughty toward him.

Miss Jane looked at all of them. "I hope that you all consider what I have said and that you don't make the same mistakes in the future," she said. "I hope that you get things right with God too, as you know that you did things He doesn't approve of."

"Yes, Miss Jane," the children replied.

"Well, that is all I have to say. You may go now."

The children slowly rose to their feet and made their way to the door. "Abel," Miss Jane called. "Please remain behind. I'd like to have a few words with you privately."

Abel, mystified, returned to his seat while the others made their way outside the school, curious about what Miss Jane had to say to Abel in private.

Miss Jane began to speak once the others were clearly out of the building. "Abel," she said. "I wanted to talk to you particularly because I believe that you must understand how Burt feels the most, for you have been in his shoes."

Abel looked at her in bewilderment, not understanding what she meant.

"I remember a time," Miss Jane said, smiling slowly, "when I had quite a different Abel in my class—a defiant, rebellious one who made out as if he had no feelings and didn't care about anything. And indeed, it was quite difficult having him in my class."

Abel turned red as he remembered how horrible he had once been. He remembered how mean and rude he had been to the others, especially to Miss Jane.

"But now," Miss Jane said, smiling an even bigger smile, "he has changed from the inside out. He is now a wonderful Abel—strong, bold, courageous, honest, and dependable, and I love having him in my class."

Abel turned even redder at the unexpected compliment. He didn't think he was as good as Miss Jane thought he was. He had been awful to Burt. But he did enjoy the compliment, and he thought that it was worth leaving his old ways to have Miss Jane compliment him like that.

"However," Miss Jane continued, "you still have a lot to work on, Abel. The tests will keep coming, and you will either pass or fail."

Abel looked down. "I didn't do very well on the 'Burt the Bully' test," he said gloomily.

"No, I'm afraid you didn't. I hope you will change your ways, though, and be a lot kinder to Burt in the future."

"It's just that Burt is so mean and such a bully," Abel grumbled.

"But you were just like him, maybe even worse," Miss Jane said. "You ought to understand how he feels."

"How?"

"Well, think about your behavior when you first came to school," Miss Jane said. "I do believe that you put on an act to hide how you really felt deep inside, didn't you?"

"Yes," Abel said, remembering. "I remember feeling...well, sort of frightened and upset." Abel frowned. He still didn't like admitting that he had felt frightened in his life, for he scoffed at fear and weakness of any kind.

"Do you think that is what Burt must have been feeling," Miss Jane asked him, "and that his bullying and don't-care attitude was just put on to hide it?"

"Well...I guess so," Abel replied hesitantly. It was hard to imagine Burt feeling like that...but then again, he had felt like that, and he had probably been worse than Burt.

"And do you think that Burt felt sad and hurt when you treated him how you did?"

"Yes. I...I'm sorry we did all those things to him, Miss Jane. Really, I am."

Miss Jane nodded. "Abel," she said, "1 Samuel 16:7 talks about how God looks at each person differently than we do. We might look at someone's appearance or the way they behave, but God doesn't. He looks at the heart. God knows each person better than we do and sees them for who they really are. That is why we must ask Him to give us a heart like His and to help us see everyone through His eyes. Do you understand?"

"Yes, Miss Jane," Abel said fervently. "I understand. I'll be kinder to Burt from now on, and I'll never forget to look at everyone through God's eyes. I bet I'll see people quite differently if I do!"

Chapter Fifteen: A New Burt

"Therefore, if anyone is in Christ, he is a new creation. The old has passed away; behold, the new has come." 2 Corinthians 5:17

The students were much nicer to Burt from that day onward, especially Abel. Abel took it upon himself to befriend Burt, and though Burt didn't show it, he was rather grateful someone gave him a cheery grin now and then and tried his best to start a cheery conversation with him.

Indeed, Abel's efforts were certainly praiseworthy, but unfortunately, he didn't get much from the obstinate Burt. He answered all Abel's questions with one-word answers, but most of the time he just ignored everything and everybody.

"What is your favorite subject?" Abel asked him once.

"I don't like anything that has to do with school," Burt replied curtly.

Abel sat and mused for a while, trying his hardest to come up with another question that would develop into a more lengthy conversation.

"What do you like doing in your spare time?" he asked again, crossing his fingers.

To Abel's surprise, Burt's face brightened, and his eyes sparkled. "I enjoy riding horses," he said. "I love it. But I can't do it anymore, as I don't have a horse."

"Did you have a horse before you moved in with Parson Davy?" Abel asked.

"Easy, boy! Woah, easy there! Calm down, old fella!" said Burt

Burt's face fell. "I did," he replied. "His name was Lightning, and he was the best horse in the world."

"What happened to him?"

"I had to sell him." Burt abruptly turned around, making it clear to Abel that he didn't want to talk anymore, and Abel left, sighing over his bad luck.

One day, Abel and Pat were going into town together to buy some groceries for their parents. They were just coming out from Mr. Morrisby's grocery store when they heard a voice shout from not far away, "Stop that horse! Quick, stop him, stop him!"

Half a second later, a beautiful black stallion galloped past an open-mouthed Abel and Pat. The horse continued to run from its owner, never once stopping or slowing down. People shrieked and dodged out of the way, and carts and carriages came to a screeching halt. Everyone watched desperately as the horse ran on, creating total chaos in the usually sedate town.

Suddenly, Abel gave an exclamation and nudged Pat. "Oh, Pat! Isn't that Burt over there? Do look! Whatever is he doing?"

Burt, who often liked to take a stroll in town, had been walking calmly when the horse had whizzed past him like a whirlwind. Turning around, he had heard a man's voice crying in desperation for someone to stop his horse, and Burt decided to do just that. He spotted a chestnut mare tied to a pole nearby, patiently waiting for its rider to exit a store. Burt quickly untied the horse and hoisted himself onto the saddle. Soon, he had urged the horse into a gallop, and they were flying at full speed after the runaway black stallion.

Burt was soon inches behind the stallion, and he steered the mare beside him. They galloped beside each other, neck and neck for a few minutes, before Burt lunged out and grabbed the stallion's saddle horn. When he had gotten a good grip, he swung himself from the chestnut mare onto the stallion's back and quickly took control of the horse's reins, pulling in with all his might. The stallion bucked his head and swerved its body, causing Burt's leg to crash against the side of a building. Burt bit his lip, turning white with pain. "Easy, boy! Woah, easy there! Calm down, old fella!" he said in the calm, gentle voice that he used specially for horses. Burt's calm and controlled manner had an effect on the stallion, and it came to a standstill, breathing heavily. Burt ran his hand down its trembling body and whispered comfortingly into its ear.

"Wow! Did you see that?" Pat said to Abel in amazement. "Burt's a hero!"

Pat, Abel and the rest of the crowd ran toward Burt and the stallion. But Burt heard none of their praise, for having been quite exhausted and unable to bear the pain in his throbbing leg, he had fainted, and everyone found him hunched over and unmoving. The doctor was called for as gentle arms lifted the boy from the stallion's back. The town was soon buzzing with the news, and everyone wanted to know where the "brilliant young horseman" lived.

****

Burt was not able to come back to school the next day. The doctor had confirmed that Burt's leg was broken, and Burt was ordered to stay in bed and rest until he had recovered enough to go back to school.

The news of Burt's heroic deed spread like wildfire through Miss Jane's school and the community, and visitors showed up continually at Parson Davy's house to visit Burt.

Abel was one of the visitors, taking with him a book and a box of chocolates for Burt.

Burt was sitting up in bed, and Abel was amazed to see the change in him. His face had brightened considerably, and his eyes sparkled with friendliness.

"Hello, old thing," Abel said, giving him a smile. "How's the hero doing?"

"Stop it!" Burt said, blushing. "Abel, it's so good to see you! How are you doing? I've been longing to go back to school."

"Really?" Abel asked with surprise. "That's the last thing I'd expect you to say, Burt!"

Burt colored with embarrassment. "I know," he said humbly. "I've had a lot of time to think, sitting here in bed. I was not at all nice to any of you, and yet, when news got around that I had broken my leg, I have had so many visitors from school! You all are so nice, and I see now that I've been behaving very badly. I mean to change that, you see."

"I bet you will," Abel said, liking this new Burt already. "You'll be the nicest kid in town!"

Burt grinned. "How is it that even when I was such a bully, you all were so kind to me? You were rather mean at first, but I deserved it. You became awfully kind all of the sudden, though, and I've always wondered why."

Abel nodded. "We *were* mean, but then we all realized that Jesus would not treat you that way, and we were not at all behaving like followers of Jesus. We decided to follow Jesus' example and be kind to you, just like He would."

Burt listened intently. "It was awfully hard for me to settle down in a school, you see," he told Abel. "I had never been to a school before. A private tutor taught me at home. I didn't have any friends, just Lightning. When Uncle Davy took me in, he said that going to school could do me a lot of good. But I didn't like the idea of it at all. It made me feel frightened."

Abel nodded. "I understand. I felt exactly like you did when I first came to school, and acted kinda like you did, too!"

"Really?" Burt asked with surprise. "What made you change?"

"Jesus," Abel replied. "He's the best thing that happened to me."

"Tell me more about Jesus," Burt said eagerly.

Abel shared the gospel with Burt, and in that little, quiet bedroom, Burt accepted Jesus as his Lord and Savior.

"This is the best day of my life," Burt laughed happily.

"The day's not over yet," Abel said with a big grin. "There's something I've got to tell you."

"What's that?"

"The owner of the horse you brought to a halt yesterday is willing to give the horse to you as a gift of gratitude. He said he knows no one who could control that horse as you did, and he'll be glad to get rid of him, for he's quite hard to manage. So you see, Burt, you'll have a horse of your very own again!"

Burt clapped his hands and gave a shout of glee. "Oh Abel!" he cried. "Today just gets better and better!"

****

"Three cheers for Burt! Hip, hip, hurrah!" cried Abel, followed by all the other students.

Burt once again appeared at the entrance of the school, leaning on a crutch for support. This was a different Burt, though. He was smiling pleasantly, his eyes sparkling with excitement. He blushed slightly with embarrassment as he hurried to his seat. Immediately, Prissy stood up and handed him a small gift wrapped in pretty wrapping paper with an elegant bow on top.

"A present to you, from the entire class," she said with a smile.

"Don't worry," Pat said with a cheeky grin, "it's not a snake!"

The class burst out laughing, Burt laughing the loudest of all. Carefully, he tore the wrapping paper and gasped as he saw what his gift was. In his hands, he held the prettiest pocketbook Bible he had ever seen.

"Thank you," he said, "this...this is the best present I've ever had!"

Miss Jane smiled and patted him on the shoulder. "Why don't we start class by having you read something to us, Burt?" she asked.

Burt nodded and, with delicate fingers, opened the Bible and flipped through the pages. As his clear voice filled the room, five children looked at each other and grinned. The "Burt the Bully" problem had been solved.

Chapter Sixteen: Shining the Light

"In the same way, let your light shine before others, so that they may see your good works and give glory to your Father who is in heaven." Matthew 5:16

Weeks had passed since Burt's arrival at school. Burt had made many new friends, but his very best friend was God. He spent many afternoons with Abel and Parson Davy talking about God, school, and life in general.

Everyone in school accepted Burt for who he really was, and he soon became a favorite. Burt excelled as a student, and one week, he was even top of the class!

Claire lent him numerous books from her collection, out of the kindness of her heart. Poor Burt was often forced to read Shakespeare when he badly wanted to ride Thunder. But he didn't complain for fear that he would hurt Claire's feelings.

Prissy sewed him all kinds of clothing—that more than often didn't fit correctly. But Burt wore them cheerfully to school, despite receiving many stares.

Charlie gave him chocolates, bubble gum, and many other candies, although it pained his dear heart terribly. He hid in his room most days and cried his heart out. Poor Charlie! But then again, too many sweets were not good for the chubby little boy!

Pat and Burt spent many enjoyable hours together with Thunder. Pat, who was fond of all animals, took a special liking to Thunder, and Thunder loved him back. At first, Burt felt uncomfortable sharing his best friend with anyone, and he even felt a little jealous. But after noticing how affectionate Pat was with his horse, Burt let him ride Thunder whenever he felt like it. The two boys often had hour-long conversations about their beloved horse. During these times, the others learned that it was best to keep away, or else they would be forced to listen to their boring horse talk.

It was Tuesday afternoon, and Claire was sitting in the library with her nose buried in a Shakespeare book, like usual. She was supposed to be doing her Math homework—but putting Claire and Math together was like asking a mouse and a lion to be friends. On the other hand, separating Claire from her precious books was as difficult as asking Charlie to forsake his sweets.

Absorbed in the book, Claire barely heard Miss Jane come into the house and make her way into the library. Only when Miss Jane came to the library was Claire aware of her presence.

Claire looked up, prepared to see a frowning Miss Jane wagging a finger at her and forcing her to do her dreadful Math problems. But instead, much to her surprise, Claire saw a rather distressed looking Miss Jane, who sunk into a nearby chair with an enormous sigh.

"What's wrong, Miss Jane?" Claire asked with concern. "You look worse than if you had solved one hundred algebra equations!"

Miss Jane laughed despite herself. "Oh, Claire, I've just got a letter from my cousin Evelyn who lives in New York. She's invited me to her wedding that is to take place next week. I badly want to go, for little Evie is such a dear, and we've been like sisters for ever so long. The Ministry of Education said they'll find a substitute teacher to take over at school if I do go, but I don't want to leave when you're just about to take your final exams."

"Oh, you needn't worry about us, Miss Jane," Claire said, looking at her motherly teacher with affection. "We'll be as good as gold for the substitute."

THE SCHOOL OF LIFE

"Oh, I know you will, dear," Miss Jane said earnestly. "I'm just nervous about how the substitute will treat you! I don't want to leave you in bad hands, you know."

"Oh, don't worry!" Claire said, heartily. "We'll manage. I bet the substitute will be one of the sweetest, kindest people that ever lived!"

"Well, I do hope so," Miss Jane said. "I guess I'm attending the wedding, then?"

"You sure are," Claire replied.

****

Monday came, and the substitute teacher arrived. Immediately, a hush fell upon all the students as they gazed in wonder at their teacher.

She was a tall, heavy-set woman, who towered above the students from what seemed like a hundred feet up. She wore a large frown on her face that seemed to be as long as the Nile. Her black hair was pulled tightly into a bun that rested on the top of her round head, and her sharp black eyes noticed everyone and everything, from an ant on the floor to Charlie's fudge-smudged face.

The substitute strode up to the teacher's desk, the earth seeming to tremble with each step her large feet took. She plopped into the chair and glared at the students, rapping her fingers on the desk. "Good morning, students," she said in a low, rumbling kind of voice.

The morning classes went smoothly. The substitute teacher's name was Mrs. Outlaw, although the students didn't believe her at first. Unfortunately, Charlie, who couldn't remember names very well, landed into much trouble because of Mrs. Outlaw's name.

The class had come in from their lunch break and was working on Math when Charlie raised his hand to ask a question.

"Excuse me, Mrs. In-law, I am rather stuck on problem thirty-three. Could you please teach it to me again?" Something about Charlie's manner seemed to irritate the substitute.

"My name is not Mrs. In-law," she said harshly.

"Good morning, students," she said in a low, rumbling kind of voice

"Oh! I'm so sorry, Mrs. Lawless!" Charlie said sincerely, giving a sheepish grin. "You really must forgive me. I have a poor memory, you see. I'm dreadful with names!"

That was enough for the substitute. She rose to her full height and stormed toward Charlie. Her face was red with fury, and her eyes sparkled with rage. She breathed fire from her nostrils and looked ready to fly through the ceiling (according to Charlie, at least). Charlie gulped and sank into his chair. The substitute leaned over, her face right in front of Charlie's.

"My name is not Mrs. In-law, Mrs. Lawless, or anything else!" she said in a loud voice. "My name is Mrs. *Out*law, and I shall not allow cheeky boys like you to make fun of it!"

Charlie nearly fainted, while the rest of the class gasped.

"Er...I'm so sorry, Mrs....Mrs....," Charlie hesitated.

"Outlaw!" the substitute bellowed.

Mrs. Outlaw turned on her heel, and Charlie quickly popped a chocolate into his mouth to calm himself, receiving sympathetic glances from the class.

The rest of the day was quite dreadful. Mrs. Outlaw proved to be a very hard person to please. If you handed in a Math paper and all your answers were correct, Mrs. Outlaw would take points off for neatness. The highest grade received for composition that day was a 'C,' earned by a mortified Claire, who usually received an 'A' for any written work. But it was hardest for Charlie. He was scolded non-stop, and he was asked hard questions that no one knew the answers to, getting unfairly reprimanded when he couldn't answer correctly. He kept getting the lowest grades in the class, leading him to eat even more candy than usual to help ease his mind. It was obvious that Mrs. Outlaw disliked him the most because she thought he had been making fun of her name.

After what seemed like an eternity, the school day was over, and the class thankfully flooded outside. Abel, Burt, Pat, Charlie, Claire and Prissy got together in the schoolyard.

"Well! Why ever did *she* have to come and teach us?" Prissy asked, her gentle temperament giving way to unusual anger.

"Why does she have to be so mad at us?" Pat said. "I don't see what's wrong with our class. We're a pretty good bunch. Most people like us."

"She's probably mad at us because of me," Charlie said, turning red.

"That was silly of you, Charlie," Abel scolded. "She specifically told the class that her name was Mrs. Outlaw. How could you be so forgetful?"

"I do think that's unfair, Abel," Prissy said loyally. "It was an accident. We might have very easily done the same."

Claire giggled. "It was funny, though, wasn't it? I mean, what an unusual name to have!"

The others looked at her grimly. "I didn't think it was very funny," Charlie said soberly.

"Well, yes, of course, Charlie, er...it must have been very painful for you." Despite her efforts, Claire started giggling, her eyes gleaming with fun. "But just imagine how Mrs. Outlaw and her family sign their Christmas cards! Merry Christmas. Love, the Outlaws.' Ha, Ha!"

The others looked at each other and shook their heads. "Claire, this is no time for laughing," Abel said seriously. "We must do something about Mrs. Outlaw. She's ruining our grades!"

"Well, whatever we do, let's please not do anything unpleasant," said Prissy, who hated to do anything mean.

"We mustn't worry Miss Jane with our troubles," Pat said. "It would bother her, and she wouldn't be able to enjoy the wedding. But we do need a grown-up to help us. Who do we ask?"

"Parson Davy!" Burt said promptly. "He'll know what to do."

"Yes, of course!" Abel exclaimed. "Parson Davy! How about we all go to his house right now?"

The others agreed. The six children determinedly made their way to Parson Davy's house, which was only ten minutes away from the school. When they arrived, Burt went up to the doorstep and opened the door.

"Uncle Davy! Are you home?" he called. "I'm back from school with Abel and a couple of friends of mine. We'd like to speak with you about something if you don't mind."

The children heard quick footsteps and saw Parson Davy appear at the doorway. "Hello, children!" he greeted them,

THE SCHOOL OF LIFE

giving a friendly grin. "What brings you here on this sunny, most glorious day? And my, don't you all look solemn!"

"We've come to discuss a most serious matter with you," Abel declared, sounding very grown-up. "We need your advice, you see. We're in quite a predicament."

"I see, I see," Parson Davy said, grabbing his hat. He stepped out onto the doorstep and closed the door behind him. "What is this big predicament of yours?"

"Miss Jane is away attending her cousin's wedding," Claire explained. "That's bad enough on its own, but now we have to deal with an awful substitute at school who is ruining all our grades. She's a most grumpy person, so dreadfully sour all the time, and boy, does she yell! It's horrible to sit in school all day with her teaching us, and we just don't know what to do."

Parson Davy nodded. "It must be very trying for you."

"We did nothing to upset her, except call her by another name on accident," Pat said. "We don't see why she's in such a foul mood, and there seems no way for us to put her in a good one."

"What do you advise us to do?" Prissy asked. "Our school has turned into a downright lion's den!"

Parson Davy was thoughtful. Finally, he snapped his fingers.

"Follow me," he said, walking away from his house. "I know the solution to your problem."

The others followed Parson Davy, curious as to where he was taking them.

"Where are we going, Parson?" Claire asked.

"You'll see," Parson Davy said with a smile.

They walked several miles before they came to a store with a sign above that said "The McConnell Jewelry Shop, Inc."

"So we've come here!" Abel exclaimed in surprise. "Whatever for? I'm not that crazy about jewels, Parson Davy."

Parson Davy laughed. "You needn't worry Abel, I don't like jewelry that much either. But there's something in here that I want to show you."

The children followed Parson Davy inside the shop as he led the way to a table that stood near the window, with tiny diamonds on it all set in a row, gleaming and sparkling in the light.

"Oh! Aren't they lovely!" exclaimed Prissy with the utmost admiration.

The children 'oohed' and 'aahed' over the little stones. The diamonds were certainly very pretty.

"Do you know why these diamonds appear beautiful?" Parson Davy asked.

Claire gave him a puzzled look. "Parson Davy, they're diamonds! Diamonds are always beautiful."

Parson Davy shook his head. "In the dark, a diamond is just an ordinary stone, quite unattractive on its own. But when you take a diamond and shine a beam of light on it, it sparkles and glitters. Its value comes from the way it behaves in the light. It is the light escaping from the diamond that makes it attractive to people like you and me, and we find it extremely precious."

Burt furrowed his brow. "This is indeed important information for us all to know, Uncle, but I still don't see what it has to do with Mrs. Outlaw."

Parson Davy smiled. "I think that we all should try to be more like diamonds, Burt. We should let God's light shine through us into the lives of others. When we are filled with God's light, we gain true value. We can guide others to the true God when they see a clear difference in us."

"I see," Pat said slowly. "Maybe if we shine God's light by being kind, loving, and patient, Mrs. Outlaw might notice and not be so grumpy anymore."

Parson Davy nodded. "Exactly! Instead of acting angry and bitter, be kind and loving, and you'll find that shining God's light does make a difference around you."

"You're right, Parson Davy," Claire said, a look of determination coming over her small face. "We will all let God's light shine brightly through us, and we'll sparkle like diamonds for Jesus!"

****

The children were indeed little diamonds from that day onward—in their opinion at least. Mrs. Outlaw didn't seem to think so. She was still grumpy. But perhaps she felt a little better, because she didn't yell as often.

It was Saturday morning, and Claire was in town with a shopping list from Mrs. Thompson, with whom she had been staying while Miss Jane was away.

Claire was just about to leave Mr. Morrisby's store when she heard a woman with a loud voice saying something important to the clerk at the counter. Unable to restrain herself, she stopped and listened while pretending to be deeply interested in a bag of flour.

"All these things I'm buying are for Lucille Outlaw," the woman said, as if it was necessary for the clerk to know. "Poor Lucille. Her mother's just starting to recover from a bad illness, and Lucille's been looking after her every day and every night, with hardly a minute to rest."

The clerk didn't seem very interested in the life of Miss Lucille Outlaw. "That'll be twelve dollars, please," she said, waiting for her payment.

The woman opened her purse and drew out the money, talking all the while. "Lucille was always such a jolly thing, but slogging to make her mother comfortable ruined her. What she needs is a good rest, but Lucy won't hear of it. When she's not with her mother, she's busy teaching to pay for her mother's needs and doctor visits. She's a fine teacher, that woman is, when she's in her right mind. I feel sorry for the children she's teaching now, though. She's awfully kind, but she's got such a temper. Fault of all the Outlaws, you know. I suppose it was just passed down to her."

The woman gathered her things from the counter and made her way out of the shop, much to the clerk's relief.

Claire followed her just in time to see the women drop a package. Claire quickly ran and picked it up.

"Thank you, my dear," the woman said with a smile. She reached her hand towards the package and dropped another one in the process.

Claire smiled. "You are carrying so many things, ma'am. Would you like me to carry some things for you?"

"You are a dear!" the woman said, depositing half of her things onto Claire's outstretched arms.

She suddenly frowned. "You don't expect me to pay ya, do you? If you do, just run along!"

"Oh no, ma'am. I'll be happy to do it just because I want to."

"Well, Lucille's mother's house is quite a distance from here."

"Oh, that's all right. I like walks!"

They started, with the woman—whose name was Mrs. Baker—talking nonstop. Claire, who could be a chatterbox herself, took a liking to Mrs. Baker.

"I'm helping Lucille by taking care of her mother this week. The doctor says that Lucille is much too overworked and could do with a good rest. I finally persuaded her to take this week off while I looked after her mother. It was hard work, as you can imagine, for that Outlaw woman is as stubborn as a mule! Still, she finally consented, and I'm making sure she gets a well-deserved rest. I don't think one week is quite enough time for her to recover, though."

Mrs. Baker sighed. "I'm quite a busy woman too. I've got a pretty tight schedule as it is, and taking care of Lucille's mother just tops it all off! Lucille's mother is a dear, but you know how hard it is to care for someone who can't take one step out of bed."

While Mrs. Baker was talking, an idea had formed in Claire's head. Her eyes began to sparkle, and she looked eagerly at Mrs. Baker.

"Mrs. Baker! My friends and I from school have formed a club called 'Helping Hands.' We like to go around doing things for people and helping them when they need it. Would you like it if every day after school this week, we came and helped you take care of Mrs. Outlaw's mom? We can help you clean the house, cook, and do lots of other things, too!"

Mrs. Baker's face brightened, and she flashed a grateful smile. "Oh, you little lamb!" she exclaimed. She was fond of using such expressions, with "lamb," "dear," and "honey pie" being her favorites. "That would be wonderful! I would really appreciate

THE SCHOOL OF LIFE

it. Oh, you blessed child! Wouldn't Lucille just love to hear about you and your friends?"

"Oh, no, please," Claire said quickly, "you needn't tell Mrs. Outlaw anything about us. We'll be happy just to help her mother."

"Just as you like, sugar," Mrs. Baker replied with twinkling eyes. "You're a modest one, aren't you? They're always the best!"

From that day, the Helping Hands club fell into the routine of helping Mrs. Baker take care of Mrs. Outlaw's mother every day after school. There was always something to be done, and the children worked diligently and cheerfully until words like "lambs" and "dears" just rolled off of Mrs. Baker's tongue! Everything went smoothly, and the children got along quite well with Mrs. Outlaw's mother...well, except for Claire. Both had hot tempers and liked to speak their minds. But Grandma Outlaw was quick to apologize and tried so hard to set things right that Claire couldn't help but go back and work for her. So, the two of them would be angels from that very minute until, of course, another tempest arose, which was usually within the next five minutes.

One day, Abel and Burt were busy raking leaves in Grandma Outlaw's yard and were having quite a cheery conversation.

"Sometimes I wish I were a leaf, dancing in the wind, so swift and free!" Abel said, leaning against his rake and watching a green summer leaf fall to the ground.

Burt laughed. "You're quite poetic, aren't you?" he said. "Anyway, you don't have to be a leaf to feel swift and free. I feel like that whenever I'm riding Thunder!"

"You do look very nice when you ride Thunder," Abel observed. "As joyous as a ray of sunlight, as refreshing as a cool summer breeze, and as tranquil as moonlit waters."

Burt laughed again. "I say! What's gotten into you, Abel? You sound like Claire. You're not usually like this...Oh!" Burt said as an idea suddenly popped into his head. "You're preparing for our English test on Monday, aren't you?"

Abel nodded his head wearily. "I've just got to get a good grade. If I don't..."

"Oh no! Abel, look!"

Burt had turned deathly pale, and he grabbed Abel's arm. "Oh, Abel! Isn't that Mrs. Outlaw in that buggy?"

Abel looked to where Burt's trembling finger pointed and saw a woman in a buggy coming speedily down the dirt road toward the house.

"I say, what do we do?" Abel asked, his voice shaking.

"I suppose we'd better tell the others and hide," Burt answered in an equally shaky voice.

"My legs aren't moving!"

"Mine aren't either! They've turned into jelly!"

By this time, of course, Mrs. Outlaw had reached the house, and she looked at the boys in surprise. That didn't last long, however, for as soon as the boys' legs had stopped shaking, they began to race across the yard like guilty criminals.

"Now, you boys just wait!" Mrs. Outlaw cried with rage, bounding out of the buggy. "Just what do you think you're doing on my mother's property? I'll report you to the Sherriff for this, and next time, you'll think twice about trespassing!"

Mrs. Baker, Claire, Prissy, Pat and Charlie appeared from inside the house, staring at Mrs. Outlaw in surprise. They had heard someone shouting and had come in a rush to see what all the hullaballoo was about. The girls were covered in flour from helping Mrs. Baker cook, while the boys, who had been dusting, now appeared with their dusters still in hand.

"Lucille! What a surprise to see you here!" Mrs. Baker exclaimed.

"Is it a surprise if a daughter visits her mother who is just recovering from an illness?" Mrs. Outlaw demanded.

"Oh, indeed not, but I thought you were taking this week off to recover! You know that once you step into this house you'll find something or the other to do," Mrs. Baker answered, brushing away flour from her apron.

"Will you please explain to me, Margaret, what these children are doing here?" Mrs. Outlaw said. "I expect them to leave this house at once and never set a foot in it again! You hear that, kids? LEAVE!"

"Lucille Outlaw, I'm amazed at you!" Mrs. Baker exclaimed reproachfully. "You have no idea how much these kids have helped me take care of your mother. They're such dears! They've been dusting, raking, cooking, and cleaning. They're sugarplums, yes they are, and you should be grateful! I've never known kids like these, and boy, I wish every single person I know behaved like how they do!"

Something about Mrs. Outlaw seemed to change. Her eyes softened, and she looked at Mrs. Baker in confusion. "They...they've been taking care of my mother?" she asked in a hushed voice.

"Indeed they have, the blessed honey pies," Mrs. Baker said, nodding triumphantly. "What have you to say to that, Lucille?"

Mrs. Outlaw stood in amazement. Her face broke into a smile that changed her appearance remarkably. She looked so kind and pretty that the children gazed at her in astonishment.

"Oh, I don't know what to say!" Mrs. Outlaw exclaimed, dabbing her eyes with a handkerchief. "I am so sorry for jumping to conclusions and yelling like that. I really *am* amazed. I was so worried about my mother that I've come off as a grumpy and most disagreeable person these last few weeks. I do hope you can forgive me. Oh, you children have such good hearts! How you could put up with me and then take care of my mother afterward, I don't know!"

Prissy, who was easily touched, went and laid a hand on Mrs. Outlaw's arm.

"It's all right, Mrs. Outlaw," she said, with a smile. "We are very glad to help your mom, and we hope that she recovers soon."

"Yeah," Abel said, walking over with Burt. "We understand how hard things are for you, Mrs. Outlaw. We'll be glad to continue helping you and your mom in whatever way you like, if you want us to."

"I'm sorry I got your name wrong the first time we met," Charlie said, a look of pain crossing his face. "I'm afraid we got off to a very bad start."

Mrs. Outlaw threw her head back and laughed at this last statement. "I'm afraid I'm the one who should be sorry, Charlie," she said. "I was mad at that time...but now I see that I was really in the wrong. You can't help it if Outlaw's your name, now, can you?"

The others smiled. The rest of the day was spent helping each other and forgiving each other, mending sore hearts and destroying bitter feelings. Mrs. Outlaw felt her worries melt away as she saw the labors the little hands around her did so willingly. Her anxiety was replaced by a feeling of gratitude as she saw that there were people who cared. Through all the loving deeds the children did that day, Mrs. Outlaw was able to see the heart of our Savior, who sends friends our way to help bear our burdens while leading and guiding us with the light of his love.

And what did the six children learn that day? They learned that it is best to shine the light of Jesus in the midst of darkness. They learned that only reflecting the light of Jesus can drown out all anger and strife. To share God's love with others is the greatest thing you can do, for His love is a sea that flows with mercy and grace, free for anyone to wade in its deep waters.

True love is Christ; Christ is the light of the world; and we, His children, find our purpose in living as channels of His love and reflectors of His light.

Chapter Seventeen: Steering the Tongue

"If we put bits into the mouths of horses so that they obey us, we guide their whole bodies as well...So also the tongue is a small member, yet it boasts of great things. How great a forest is set ablaze by such a small fire!" James 3:3 and 3:5

Claire stomped across Miss Jane's front yard, fuming, with red cheeks, fiery eyes, and a frown on her face. She looked like a regular thundercloud, contrasting badly with the beautiful, sunshiny day.

Burt, who was taking a stroll past Miss Jane's house just then, stopped and looked in surprise at Claire. It was unusual to see the usual cheerful little cricket looking like a cat stuck in the rain.

"I spy with my little eyes a roaring lioness in Miss Jane's front yard!" Burt said, loud enough for Claire to hear him. "I beseech thee, oh magnificent creature, with thy flowing mane and sharp claws, to come henceforth to me, so I may turn you into the lamb you once were!" Burt finished with quite a dramatic air and a graceful gesture of his hand.

Claire felt the corners of her mouth lifting, although she tried desperately not to smile. "Don't be ridiculous, Burt," she said. "I am no roaring lioness, but perhaps I look like one. You would too if you'd been through what I have."

"And what great trials have you been through, miss?" Burt asked, walking over toward her.

"I won't tell you! You'll tease me if I do."

"I don't tease."

"Yes, you do. You did a few seconds ago when you called me a roaring lioness."

"Well, I won't tease you anymore. I'll be as serious as can be."

"You promise you won't tell a soul? If you do, I'll never speak to you again!"

"You can tell me anything. Wild horses couldn't drag it from me! C'mon, now, I'm pretty trustworthy!"

Claire sighed. "Prissy came over today, and we argued. I lost my temper with her."

"Oh, boy!" Burt exclaimed. He was very familiar with Claire's temper.

Claire crossed her arms. "I'm very upset with myself for losing my temper, but I know I was right. Prissy was being too silly. She brought all her dolls with her and wanted to play house. I humored her for some time, but when she wanted to dress up and wear makeup, I couldn't handle it anymore. She wanted me to wear lipstick! Imagine that! Wear lipstick! You can see that I had to say something. Prissy was very mad with me afterward."

"It doesn't sound like Prissy to get upset just over lipstick," Burt said.

Claire looked at the ground, half-ashamed. "Well you see...I was so angry, I said that she was very vain and looked as frightful as her awful dolls, especially with lipstick. I called her a 'proud little peacock with a big head' and told her I'd rather play with a sensible boy."

Burt whistled. "Did you really say all that? No wonder Prissy got mad! I say..." Burt scratched his head thoughtfully. "Claire, I know you and Prissy are very different and don't see eye to eye on a lot of things, but you didn't have to be so rude about it, did you?"

Claire sighed. "I suppose you're right. When I get annoyed, words just fly out, and even before I know it, I've said something I regret. I wish I could take back what I told Prissy, but it's too late. I feel awful."

Claire sighed again. "It's just that I was already having a terrible morning to begin with. First, I tore my favorite frock climbing a tree, then I baked a cake with salt instead of sugar, and I lost my homework for class on Monday! As if that wasn't bad enough, while I was frantically looking for the homework, I spilled ink all over the notebook I was writing my latest story in. When Prissy came, I was still fretting about all the morning's happenings, I just exploded! I really couldn't hold my temper any longer. Oh, Burt, I know it's awful, but what am I supposed to do?"

Claire looked so woebegone, Burt felt like patting her head and offering her chocolate.

"Claire!" Burt said, snapping his fingers. "You know what I do when I need a little cheering up?"

"What?"

"Ride Thunder!'

"Of course."

"No, I'm serious. Riding makes you feel so much better, and it clears your mind. I was heading off to ride Thunder just now. How about you come with me? We'll have a capital time!"

Claire's eyes sparkled, and her heart gave a leap. She loved horses but hardly ever got a chance to ride them. "Well...I would love that!" she said.

"C'mon, let's go!"

The two children ran to Burt's house, where Burt let Claire ride Thunder with reins to control the horse. He was pleased when he saw Claire laughing, her braids flying in the wind and a rosy color appearing on her cheeks as the summer breeze blew in her face. Claire was a fine horsewoman, and she rode gracefully.

Claire had an enjoyable ride, for Thunder responded obediently to her light touch on the reins. Claire and Burt took turns and rode Thunder for about an hour.

"You were right, Burt," Claire said with a smile. "Riding was just the perfect solution. It made me feel a lot better."

"I told you so," Burt said.

"How you can ride bareback, I don't know...and with no reins, too! I'm glad you gave me reins to steer Thunder with.

Thunder's a fine horse. He responded to my steering so obediently! I'm quite fond of him, he was so easy to manage."

Burt eyes were thoughtful, and he suddenly snapped his fingers. "You know, this reminds me of something Miss Jane taught us a few weeks ago," he said.

"What do you mean, Burt?"

"Well, what would you have thought if Thunder was rebellious to your commands and bucked and kicked, always running in the opposite direction from which you steered him?"

Claire scratched her chin. "I would have thought Thunder was a most disagreeable horse, and I wouldn't have enjoyed the ride much. It would have been dangerous for both me and Thunder."

"Why would it have been dangerous for Thunder?"

"Well, suppose there had been a tree or something right in Thunder's path, and I had tried to steer him away from it. If Thunder didn't obey me and went his own way, it would have been a total catastrophe!"

Burt nodded. "Exactly. You know, Claire, I think we all should be like Thunder. Remember what Miss Jane said? Words can be used to help and encourage or to tear down and cause hurt. We should let Jesus 'steer' our tongues in the same way Thunder let you steer him."

Claire thought for a while, then smiled. "You're right, Burt," she said. "I've done enough 'horsing around' with my words. I better hand over the reins of my tongue to the one who can control it the best.

A resolute look came over Claire's face. "I should go and apologize to Prissy right away. She's such a good friend, I know she'll forgive me, though I don't deserve it. You're a good friend too, Burt, to gently point out that I was wrong and point me to Jesus. Thanks for the steering lesson."

"No problem," Burt replied with a grin.

Chapter Eighteen: The End of the Year

"Delight yourself in the Lord, and he will give you the desires of your heart." Psalm 37:4

The end-of-the-year final exams were fast approaching, and Miss Jane was really cracking the whip. Every student prayed earnestly that he or she would make it across the finish line alive. It was difficult to sit in a classroom and study when the summer holidays were so close.

"Oh dear, oh dear! The Math finals will be the end of me!" Prissy cried, trying in vain to solve an algebra equation.

"I'm sure looking forward to the English exam," Abel said sarcastically.

Burt laughed. "I'm sure you'll do fine, Abel. You've been practicing your adjectives for ever so long, you ought to do well on the creative writing portion."

"Do you think so?"

"No. Your grammar still needs working on."

Claire bit her pencil. "Geometry is so disagreeable, isn't it? I'm dying to read a good book, but I've got to finish these problems before I do. It's agony!"

"Well, here's a delightful book you can read once you've finished," Pat said, tossing her a book.

Claire picked it up and made a face as she read the title. "'Facts about Snakes.' Really, Pat! Do you think I'd be interested in a book like this?"

Pat shrugged. "It might help you on the Science exam."

Charlie sighed and looked at the candy wrappers around him. "I've eaten about one hundred peppermint drops, and I still can't remember my parts of speech!" he said woefully.

"You should probably try eating the wrappers now," Abel said, earning himself a playful punch.

"If only summer would come!" Prissy groaned. "I'm longing to make myself a new outfit, but I have to worry about the exams instead! It's horrid if you ask me."

"Dreadful," Claire agreed. "Absolute agony, as I said before."

"Will you please be quiet?" Charlie pleaded. "My head's gone all fuzzy in this hot weather, and you chatterboxes keep distracting me even more!"

The discussion ended for the time being, as all the children went back to the task at hand. They all liked to study together at Miss Jane's house when they were out of school for the day, even though it was tempting to talk to each other. The quietness of the house provided a good atmosphere for them to study in.

Poor children! They had a hard time those few weeks, for anxiety made their tempers short, leading to quite a few squabbles. Indeed, their behavior was not at its best—horrific, you might even say—but their intentions were good. They all badly wanted to do well on the tests for their school and make Miss Jane proud.

The days crawled by, and the students finally found themselves sitting in a silent classroom as Miss Jane handed out the exams. To their surprise, the class found the papers quite easy, for Miss Jane had done a praiseworthy job of teaching them. Everyone remained calm, except for Prissy, who was always likely to go into hysterics. But even she did well, considering that she did not chew her pencils or cry on her exam papers.

At last, the exams were over, and the class waited anxiously for their scores. My, what a hullabaloo there was when they came!

"Hurrah! I've done it! I say, Burt, I've done it!" Abel cried, clutching his friend in glee. "I've passed the English exam, and with good grades too!"

Burt thumped Abel till he coughed. "Good job, Abel. I am proud of you! Guess what? I've passed the English exam too! I've passed all the other tests as well. Isn't it marvelous?"

Abel and Burt linked arms and did a barn dance, causing the rest of the class to laugh with amusement.

Claire waved her papers madly about and threw them in the air. "Ha!" she cried in a triumphant voice, giving her geometry paper a scorching glare as it fell to the floor. "I've defeated you, you mathematical enemy! You thought you could get the better of me, didn't you? But no! You did not! Ha!"

Prissy anxiously looked at her scores and began to cry hysterically. "I've passed!" she said in a choked voice, burying her face in her hands. "I've actually passed!"

"There, there. It's nothing to be upset about," Charlie said, patting her shoulder comfortingly. He could never understand the concept of shedding tears of joy.

"Oh, Charlie," Prissy said, wiping away her tears. "Don't be ridiculous! I'm not upset, I'm happy! I'm the happiest girl in the world. Did you pass all your exams, too?"

"Oh, of course," Charlie said matter-of-factly. This was not surprising, for hardly anything caused him to get excited.

Pat was all smiles. "Yippee!" he cried, leaping so high that his most agitated pet frog, George, found himself bouncing uncontrollably in Pat's pocket. "Miss Jane, I've passed! Would you have thought it possible, Miss Jane?"

"Definitely not!" Miss Jane said, pretending to be shocked, her twinkling eyes betraying her. "Did you really pass, Pat? Unbelievable!"

Everyone in the class had passed. Claire had won the Best Written Composition Award and was delighted. Pat was top in Science and had passed the test with flying colors. Abel got the highest score in Geometry, for he liked Math and was good at it. Burt beat the class in Geography, and his test score was almost perfect. Prissy came out top in History. Charlie was well rewarded, for, after hours of studying his parts of speech, he had won the English Grammar Award and was pleasantly surprised and delighted.

It was a very happy time for the school that day. The students all learned that if they worked their best, their diligence would be rewarded by Him who blesses us day by day. If they made Christ their priority and did what was pleasing and honorable in His sight, He would uphold them with His right hand, and others would glorify Him for who He is. Even though it was only a small thing like passing their exams with excellent grades, the students all felt the sweetness of being rewarded for their work. They would carry the lovely memory of achievement from that day onward, and it would help them in the future as they conquered with zest trials much greater than an exam.

After some time of letting her students run wild, Miss Jane clapped her hands and called them all to order. When exam papers were picked up and everyone was seated calmly in their seats, the students looked expectantly at Miss Jane, who had something important to say.

Miss Jane looked around at the class and smiled her sweetest smile. "Oh children, I cannot describe to you how wonderful this year has been for me," she began. "It has been delightful to see each one of you walk and grow in the Lord. I am so glad that Christ allowed me to teach children like you, for I have learned so much from you all. Although it may seem to you that I did all the teaching and you all the learning, that's not true. I am a pupil, just like all of you, being taught patiently by my Heavenly Father. I have learned many important lessons this year through every disappointment and every joy. Our time together has ended, until next year that is, as we all break for the summer. But I want you all to remember, even on your vacation, to live every day only for your Father who dwells in heaven. Remember to spend time with your Father, for we are never done learning the many lessons He still has to teach us. Don't be discouraged when you fail or make mistakes, for your Father will always be ready to pick you up by the right hand and give you another chance. Never leave His school, dears, for it is there that we truly learn to live. It is the School of Life."

The students listened intently, each of them taking heed to Miss Jane's wise advice.

Prissy gave a little sob. "Whatever is the matter, Prissy?" Miss Jane asked.

"I didn't think of it till now...but I've just realized how much I'll miss school, and you, Miss Jane!" Prissy wholeheartedly exclaimed.

Cries rose from the students as they all got up from their seats to thank Miss Jane for teaching them and give her a departing hug.

"Miss Jane," Burt said as he thanked his teacher, "thank you so much for teaching us and investing your time into us. I didn't want to come to school at first, but I'm jolly glad I did! It's dreadful to imagine how much I would have missed. I shall miss you terribly, Miss Jane. I'm awfully glad I'm coming back next year, though!"

And so, we leave Abel, Burt, Pat, Prissy, Charlie and Claire as they depart from their precious school, taking with them the many important lessons that would be the making of them. We will see them all again, but until then, always remember, my dear friend, that there is a School of Life for all of us, taught patiently and kindly by our Heavenly Father. When the lessons are hard to learn, always turn to the One who is ready to guide us and lead us by the light of His love. And when all our tests we finally ace, we shall behold our heavenly Father face to face and hear Him say those blessed words, "Well done, my good and faithful servants."

The End

About the Author

Rachel Ambat is the author of this book. She is also my loving and fun cousin. Rachel is a beautiful person to spend time with and hang out with. She also has a sister named Christina who is equally fun. Rachel loves to write stories and be creative. She just doesn't write impressive stories, but her singing to the Lord is breathtaking as well! I just love listening to her sing. Rachel plays a whole band of instruments and she is good at them too. "The School of Life" is filled with fun and entertaining characters. Once you start this book, you'll never want to put it down. I have read this book about five times and I never get tired of reading it! When you read "The School of Life," you will feel the characters' feelings and feel like you are part of the story. Anytime is a fine time to curl up with this wonderful book!

Annelisa Stephen
(9 years old)

About the Illustrator

Emily Reich is a freelance illustrator and artist from the small town of Beloit, Ohio who started out young--doodling stories of lonely T-rex's and rainbow princesses. Since then she has moved from this to that—school to work--but always her heartlands in bringing to life the ideas and values that have been instilled in her as a child. The ability and opportunity to illustrate life at its core is a privilege she counts most dear and hopes to continue it as long as she abides here on God's green earth. Her goal is to follow her Creator in the art of expounding truth in its simplest of forms.....pictures.

Liked *The School of Life*?
Read the sequel!

Made in the USA
Columbia, SC
19 November 2021

49374543R00070